Pocket Dragons

Hannah Hunley

This book is dedicated to:

The readers who have joined along in these wild and fantastic adventures, Maddox and Lochlan Pillow, Julia and Calla Friedman, Dina Larsen, and Juliet Crites.

Pogo Katz and all my other animal guides.

Thomas O'Shaughnessy, the embodiment of Angus.

My mother and father, Brigette and Andrew Hunley.

My Grandpa John Chelberg, my ultimate inspiration.

Library of Congress Control Number:2018901833
NKP, Fairfield, CA
ISBN: 978-0692052082

First Edition, December 2017
http://www.manyworldsnovels.com

Pronunciation Guide

Isis - Eye siss

Angus - Aang gus

Frida - Free da

Azara - Az are ah

Eoghan - Oh wen

Kostya - Cost ee ah

Alastair - Al ah stare

Iah - Eye ah

Prologue

Before you embark on this adventure into the world of Pocket Dragons, there are some things that you must know.

The pocket dragons are quite interesting creatures. They've been around for thousands of years and will likely be here for thousands more. They sleep on the windowsills and roam the cobblestone streets. They perch on the rooftops alongside the sparrows and glare down at the humans introspectively. Some raid castles and escape with the load of a single coin or amulet. Some stow away on boats and wagons and others simply decide to swim and fly. There are pocket dragons that lounge in ice cream parlors and dragons that fly free in forests. In some places they are respected like kings and worshipped like gods, where in others they are chased out like pests or hunted like rodents. Whimsical doctors believe their blood is a miracle cure while wise men see that some heal on their own accord. But the most important thing to know about them is that they are never more than the size of a house sparrow.

They come in all shapes and colors as one may imagine dragons would. Desert pocket dragons sleep beneath warm sands like crocodiles in rivers. Jungle pocket dragons of vibrant colors glide between tall trees and nest inside large flowers. Royal pocket dragons perch on the shoulders of queens and kings, and arctic pocket dragons help warm up Eskimos in their yurts. In France, pocket dragons perch atop the Eiffel tower, while pocket dragons in New York do the same on the Empire State Building.

It may seem obvious enough to you why they are called pocket dragons. Yes, they are in fact, quite petite. Though they have also earned the name from their infamous tendency to travel in the pockets of unsuspecting travelers. For how else are they supposed to travel from New York to London without the generally overpriced airline tickets?

But in a world where dragons are as common as housemice, it is the unfortunate truth that many are treated as such. Some pet shops find it acceptable to sell dragons beside the geckos and snakes as if the dragons were as sentient as the lizards. But the dragons are actually very smart, and many speak the human tongue and are as educated as a typical human, though some decide to keep to their cultures and refer to the humans as the pests.

The last thing you must know about pocket dragons is that each is magical, the only magical creatures on Earth, in fact. Some breathe fire as typical dragons might, others bend elements to their will or have powers entirely unimaginable— until you witness them, that is.

So without further ado, welcome to the sizeable world of Pocket Dragons.

1

The Goddess of the Egyptians

Isis Bastet delicately sat on her little throne of gold, high above the city below. The priests were gathered around her, worshipping her. *Just as they should be, for all I've done for them this last century,* She thought contentedly. She peered down at the robed men and women, a flight of golden pyramid stairs below, pleased as they bowed and chanted. The gold of the pyramid gleamed in the light, and she enjoyed the warmth of the Egyptian sun that shone through her little glass throne room at the top of it.

She tilted a little ear forward to better hear the priests. "Thank you, oh Goddess of the Sun, for saving our lives with your gifts. Thank you, oh Goddess of the Sun, for guiding us during our trials. Thank you, oh Goddess of the Sun, for teaching us the ways that are right. Thank you, oh Goddess of the Sun..." They chanted.

The edge of her lip curved up just a slight, remembering all of the occasions in which they mentioned. It was constantly to her amusement that the humans always failed to distinguish her from her ancestors, differentiate her deeds from theirs, but she didn't mind. She just let them continue thanking her, complimenting her, admiring her... all the while resisting the food they had left in offering...

But she had to be a Goddess to them. She and all of her ancestors before her had maintained it, and she wasn't about to ruin the ruse just because she wanted a snack.

She tried not to look at the blackberry tart that waited at the top of the offering pile just outside her little palace. She could have sworn it was taunting her with its sticky sweet filling, just calling to her.

She suddenly wished that she had done less to help these people, for maybe then they wouldn't spend multiple hours a day praying to her— hours that she had to play the sharp-eyed stone-faced Goddess.

Eventually the priests moved on to things they prayed to her for. It was white noise to her by now. "Health... Wealth... Happiness..." They droned.

Then, they moved on to personal requests— things her people asked for. "Rain for my crops... Success for my child..." Just more of what she had heard before. "Return to us the missing gods…" The priests then said amongst the list.

Missing gods? This one caught her interest. *One of the dragons is missing*? She made a mental note to look into that one.

For she was not the only of the gods that helped rule this part of Egypt— there was Iah, the Moon Goddess, and Set, the God of animals. There were many more of them, all dragons trying to guide the humans. *I wonder who is missing...*

Her stomach growled, and she resisted the urge to shift on her talons. But sitting still in the heat always became difficult, so she did something that was acceptable— admiring herself.

Or at least she pretended to, if only to just stretch her neck and move her stiff tail. She peered down at her chest, at the white chestplates and the jeweled necklace resting atop them. She studied her wing, the membrane as pure a white as her chest, but would glow many other colors with the light through them. She looked over her scales, each perfect and polished, the color of gold and rich amber. She examined the white bone of her kitten-tooth sharp talons. She turned to a mirror in the wall to her left, looking at the overly ornate headdress that rested over her pearly white horns. She looked into her own eyes: a rich emerald green flecked with gold. She curled her tail over her front talons to look at that too— at the little white spikes that gilded her perfectly formed tail.

By the time she had finished her mock preening, she realized there was a strange silence around her. She peered down out to the area below, and saw that the priests had indeed left. *Finally,* she murmured mentally. She removed her headdress with her talons and set it down in a compartment underneath her throne.

She stepped down and out of her little glass palace that was her home every day for all of a few hours, and towards the offering pile. She glided down the steps on her moon white wings, making a beeline for that little blackberry tart. She could almost taste the fruity sweetness.

She landed on a piece of fruit and analyzed the tart. It was almost as big as her, so there would be no taking the whole thing with her, despite the surprising strength a pocket dragon could muster. She picked up the two ends of the round tart in her talons, raised it up a few inches... Then smashed it onto the bread loaf beneath it. The tart fractured into three uneven pieces.

She chose one wedge of the fractured tart, then, clutching it in her fore talons, set off into the air again. She couldn't eat in her palace—no, the priests were scrupulous enough to notice the crumbs. So instead, she had to find somewhere slightly more private.

She looked down at the city below as she flew, looking for a nice place to finally have her first meal that day. It was indeed modern, with cars and towering buildings and shops and humans galore. However, she and the other pocket dragon Gods and Goddesses of the desert had managed to retain some of its culture and spirit. The parts of Egypt that still worshipped the dragons were far better off than those that didn't— those had turned into dirty, criminal infested, disease ridden places where the air was so thick with pollution that the sky was gray.

But not here, *here*, her city glowed. She used her magic to heal the sick, and her wits to ensure that the untaught were taught, to make sure that her city was kept as bright and thriving as her ancestors did even before the humans came around to inventing their machines. She just had to be clever.

She finally decided on one of her favorite places to rest and eat at this time of day before attending to the rest of her duties— an obelisk in a part of the city that received little traffic. It was a tall, sleek, obsidian obelisk on a stone base with ancient hieroglyphs written in neat lines down it. Her grandmother and overseen its construction, and it told of her greatness as Goddess of the Sun. However, it was small, and not overly impressive, so it was rarely visited. The perfect place for the Goddess of the Sun to escape.

She knew her guards and the priests wouldn't like her sneaking away— they placed her in the highest security. But that was no way for a dragon to live, under human supervision every waking hour. So she made sure there were times each day when there would be no priests, no guards to watch her. Times when she could slip away.

She lifted the tart to her delicate but strong snout and took a bite of the fruity pastry. She didn't care much for the bread, but the berries she enjoyed.

Isis took her time, enjoying every moment she had to herself. To sit in silence, to just think and imagine and fantasize. She didn't think she would have ever lasted this long as

Goddess if she hadn't made time for these moments.

When she had eaten all of the blackberries from the tart, she discarded the crust on the concrete by the obelisk— there were plenty of birds around who would happily eat it.

She took a moment to flex her wings, ready to return to the sky and the pyramid and being a Goddess—

When she felt solid hands suddenly close around her.

2

Creature of The Causeway

Angus Ailyll drowsily awoke, his face and legs buried deep into something soft, wooly, and somewhat smelly.

He lifted his scaly green head, blinking the sleep from his golden eyes then staring blankly at the sea of pungent rolling fuzzy whiteness before him.

The sea of fuzzy whiteness let out a *baaaaaaaaa*. Several others proceeded to follow suit. Angus sighed and plopped his head back into the soft wool. He had fallen asleep on a sheep. Again.

They were just too comfortable.

Mobile beds the Irish pocket dragons liked to call them. The dragons were so small that they could easily conk out on one of them and have a warm, comfortable sleeping place for the night. The only disadvantage was the tendency for one to fall asleep one place, then wake up somewhere entirely different. *Ahhh... It was worth it though...* He thought contentedly.

He lifted his head to scan the area. Angus could be halfway across Ireland for all he saw. Endless fields and rolling hills of green, dotted by the occasional fluffy white sheep divided by hedges and fences and large bushy plants with orange flowers on them. The occasional building also speckled the area, and he could see a road going down the side of the pasture he was in.

But he was not, in fact, on the other side of Ireland, for sheep could only go so far in one night plus the fact that they had a limited roaming area. The causeway could be no more than a few miles from here.

The Giants Causeway was his home of sorts. He would steal scraps from the cafe or the visitor's leftovers, then he got to spend the rest of the day spooking the tourists— for by some happy chance, he had remarkable similarity to the dragon spoken of in the legend of the creation of the Giant's Causeway. His scales were multiple shades of rich green, and his glittering golden eyes accented them. His twisting horns were also gold, to match his gold glimmering chestplates. His talons were a sheer sharp black, though he mostly used them for clutching the wooly backs of sheep as he slept.

He looked again towards the other sheep, and noticed there were fewer pocket dragons napping on their backs than usual when he would get up in the morning. He had been noticing fewer dragons of late, though no one thought much of it— They weren't a clan or community, just a group of dragons that liked to sleep on the same sheep herd for safety. It wasn't uncommon for a dragon to decide they wished to leave, then do so without any notice whatsoever. Yet there were definitely fewer dragons around... *Oh no, I wonder if I've slept in...* He thought. He usually preferred to get to the Causeway early before they opened for tourists, mostly so that he could fly right in and not be seen.

Angus turned his head towards the sky to look for the position of the sun. *Aye, that's not good,* he murmured in his head as he saw the grey, cloudy sky, no sun to be seen. *That is really, really not good!* It was definitely going to rain today— and soon.

It was very difficult for a tiny creature such as himself to fly in the rain: the raindrops would splatter down on their little wings and body and force them back down the ground eventually.

If he wanted to get to the Causeway today, where he could hide in the tourist building to keep dry, he would have to leave quickly, or risk getting caught out in the middle of nowhere with no shelter from the freezing cold.

Not wasting a moment, he detangled himself from the sheep's wool and launched into the sky, furiously beating his little wings to get there before the clouds broke. The green field rolled by beneath him, no end in sight. He knew he wasn't far— he just had to keep following the field...

A raindrop splattered on his nose, but he kept flying. Then another on his back, then another on his wing...

The clouds unleashed their bounty.

Rain splattered all over him, and water was dripping down his scales. *Not good not good!* He knew he wouldn't be able to keep up flying much longer, so he angled himself for a sheep barn not too far away. Already, he could see farmers driving their livestock into the barn.

He swooped down, gliding into the open barn door above the head of the farmer without being seen. Usually humans didn't mind, but it didn't hurt to be careful. The intensified smell of sheep greeted him once inside. *By the great golden sheep this is terrible,* he mentally complained. He hovered for a moment, looking for any place that might be slightly less pungent inside the barn. Flapping his wings, he soared up into the loft, full of pleasant-smelling hay for the animals. It wasn't exactly the causeway, but it would do until the rain stopped. *Well this has been an interesting morning, hasn't it?* He thought with a sigh. *Yet there's no sense complaining about it now,* he decided.

Angus landed on the straw scattered ground, looking for a good place to settle down and hide for a while when he heard the creaking of wood behind him. He whipped around and saw the shadow of a farmer climbing the stairs to the loft in the wall.

He quickly scanned around for someplace to hide. He spotted a little box in the corner of the loft, and bolted for it, racing in the loping run of a dragon, and darted inside the box.

Clang!

And suddenly he was enveloped in darkness.

3

The Fire of the North

Frida Frostfire perched on the windowsill of the log cabin, staring out at the snowy white land around them. Evergreen trees stubbornly retained their leaves despite the cold, and some few hundred feet ahead lay a great frozen forest of them.

She didn't like the forest.

A wolf's howl pierced the air from somewhere within the mass of trees.

That was just one of the many reasons.

The forest was dangerous and massive... She could think of so many different ways that she could die out there... Eaten by wolves... Frozen into ice... Lost... Forever, eternally lost...

She felt cold fear sink into her stomach at the thought, and so she turned away to look back inside the window, to a far more comforting scene. The cabin was a simple one-room building, with a couple of chairs, a table, a bed and a roaring fire that kept the entire place warm.

It wasn't much, but it was home.

Inside, an old man was sitting in one of the chairs, a book cradled in one hand, and a pen in the other. She looked at him through the glass with something like fondness. The man's name was Kostya, and he was the only parent she had ever known.

He had told her the story many a time, whether or not she actually understood. After a long day, he would invite her to lay down in his lap as he sat before the fire as he told the tale. "My dear Frida..." He would say. He had given her that name, for in one of the human tongues, it meant *light*. Frida had never really understood this name, for other than being a breather of fire, she did not know how she was *light*.

Kostya would tell her the tale as she would fall asleep. "I remember when I found you... Just an egg in the snow, no parents in sight... I carried your egg in my pocket, thinking you had surely died..." He would recall with a smile. "When I finally found this place, I got a fire going in the fireplace and started cleaning it up... I had set your egg down atop the mantle, as an ornament, the first to my new home." The edges of his eyes always crinkled when he recalled the next thought. "And then I heard this *crack*! I was so startled that I raced to the mantle, worried that the egg had fallen. But instead, I saw you, just staring right back at me! I'll never forget being shocked at the beautiful color of your eyes, the brilliant shine of your scales..." At that point, she had usually fallen asleep.

She let her vision zone out so that she could see herself in the glass. She looked at herself, still not sure how he had seen her as beautiful. She had scales the color of ice and snow with hints of lavender, nothing impressive. The membrane of her wings was white and gray, also not very stunning. Her talons were white, nothing fascinating there... Her slightly curved horns were white with hints of indigo— again, nothing interesting. Her chestplates were of a similar coloring as her horns.

It was hard to bring herself to look into her own eyes.

She despised her eyes.

She always tried to look down, or away, to keep others from looking at them as well.

She really had no clue how Kostya had seen them as beautiful, either.

By the snow, they weren't even the same color. One was a faded cobalt color with flecks of silvery light gray, as if looking at a gem through a blizzard. The other was a soft amber tinged with red and yellow. She turned away from the glass, not wanting to stare at her own pitiful appearance any longer.

This cabin wasn't the only one in the frozen woods of Siberia. It was part of a small village composed of mainly half a dozen other cabins and some sheds all circling a large bonfire that they always kept going.

Or rather, that she always kept going. Deciding to stretch her wings, she jumped off the windowsill and glided towards the fire. She landed close by it, feeling the heat on her scales, watching the dancing flames. She took a moment, steadying herself, taking in a long, deep breath.... She felt fire forming in her core, sparking out of the magic in her blood... She unclenched her jaw and let the fire come rolling out, feeding the flame of the bonfire and keeping it strong. Dragonfire was hotter than any fire a human could craft, and so with her fires heating the village, burning in every fireplace, she kept the deadly cold of the north at bay.

It wasn't much. It was all she *could* do. She wasn't skilled at anything, she couldn't hunt or fight... Luckily for her, it was enough for the villagers, who in turn for keeping their cabins warm gave her small scraps of the game that they caught. Kostya would always feed her anyway, always saying that she was too skinny, but she was never all that hungry.

So she just fed the fires and watched the humans. Day after day. She would listen to them read and talk and watch them build and craft and go about their day.

She turned away from the bonfire and flew down the little path through the snow that led out to the woods. It was the path that the villagers would take to go out and hunt, and she often liked to perch atop a lone fence post marking the end of the village beside the path, and wait for the hunters to return. She landed herself on the frozen wooden post and watched, wondering what the hunters would bring back this time. She hoped it would be a caribou— she liked caribou.

She waited, listening to the silence of the snowy lands. The one nice thing about this place was the utter silence. She always had more than enough time to sit and think, and here there was rarely any noise to distract one from their thoughts. Occasionally a wolf howl would pierce the air, or the wind would whistle or the trees would rustle, but never more than that.

Which was why it was so strange when she heard... A call. A *dragon's* call.

Frida was the only pocket dragon in the village. She had never even seen another of her kind before, though from Kostya's stories, she knew there were more of them out there.

Her ears flicked to attention, trying to pinpoint the sound. "Grrrrhrhhhhhh...." The distant dragon moaned. It was definitely a call for help.

Frida felt rooted to the spot. The sound was coming from the forest. The forest was dangerous. She recalled from earlier that day all of the possible things that could kill her.

All of the things that could be killing that dragon in the woods.

I am no hero... She stuttered in her mind. *I can't fight off beasts or save creatures... I'm useless... All I'll do is get myself killed...*

She glanced back at the cabin, towards where Kostya would still be happily writing his book by her fire. She considered going back, to get help... *But I don't want to put Kostya in danger. I couldn't bear it if he got hurt.*

Another distant groan met her ear. *If I die... I suppose I'll have died at least trying to be brave...* She tried to tell herself. She spread her wings and pushed herself off the post and into the air, gliding for the forest. She tried to quell the rising fear in her belly, but to little avail.

She tried not to think about how far back the safe, warm cabin was. She tried not to think about the trees now towering over her, their boughs laden with snow. She just kept flying towards the sound of the distressed dragon.

She flew until she reached a mound of snow-covered boulders, beneath which she saw a dark tunnel. *Oh no... Not a dark tunnel... Not a dark tunnel... Why does there have to be a dark tunnel...*

Another dragon's cry echoed out of the tunnel, and she forced herself to walk towards it. *I must be brave, I must be brave...* She didn't feel half as confident as she told herself she was, but she continued on anyway. *It's just the dark... There's nothing to fear but fear itself...*

And so she stepped into the tunnel.

Then with a mechanical *snap*, she was swallowed by the darkness.

4

The Dragon of the Museum

Azara perched inside the rib cage of what was likely a several million year old skeleton. A dinosaur skeleton, the humans called it. A pterodactyl, to be precise. The reorganized bones were hanging above the stream of visitors below, and Azara sat on the bones of what was likely her ancient ancestor, watching them. She was nibbling on a chunk of muffin that she had snatched from the museum cafe, careful not to get crumbs on the ancient bones.

She really didn't understand *why* the humans cared so much about these bones. After all, they were more likely her ancestors than theirs.

Yet day after day, year after year, the humans flocked to the Natural History Museum of London. *Considering their comparatively short lifespans,* Azara thought as she peered down at the slowly moving mass of heads and limbs, *they spend their time on such strange things.*

It wasn't to be said that Azara didn't have an interest in history. She loved strolling the halls— out of view of the humans, usually before opening time— and studying the replicas of creatures long since their heyday and the bones of the creatures that led to the pocket dragons and the humans.

Unsurprisingly, there was a lot more on the history of the humans than there was of the pocket dragons. The dragons knew, of course, that they had been around for millennia before the arrival of bipedal apes, and that their ancestor's tiny bones would have long since disintegrated, so the humans resorted to a lot of hypotheses.

Despite their errors, it was almost amusing reading the little blocks of text they stuck on planks in front of the skeletons and replicas and pictures and seeing what they thought, what they knew, what they theorized.

Many of the texts were augmented with information provided by a dragon professor or historian— very few dragons were allowed into professions, but in certain places such as Britain, it was possible. She had even once attended a class taught at Cambridge that was led by an old pocket dragon professor. With a two-hundred year lifespan, it was not surprising that the dragon knew far more than the human professors.

She finished her muffin, careful not to leave any crumbs on the skeleton. Azara mainly made her home in the museum, wandering the halls and the cafes and the gift shoppe. She knew how to stay out of sight of the security cameras and guards. Why the cameras were keyed on dragons and not the *far* more suspicious looking humans, she still didn't understand. As if a pocket dragon could take off with a 1-ton mosasaur bone. As if a dragon would even want to.

Very few dragons dabbled with the human's lifestyle. Most dragons didn't bother with money or purchasing things... After all, why would you even need to if you could sustain yourself on insects and table scraps and wild fruits and berries?

Azara waited until there were fewer people below to notice her, then leaped off the skeleton without causing it so much as to rustle. She glided towards a window that was open just a slight, and darted through the narrow area into the brisk outside air.

The pleasant streets and roads of the city opened up before her, dotted with cars and people going about their day. Several dragons glided through the skies or perched in the trees or on the street lamps or rooftops. London probably had the highest dragon population in Western Europe. Unsurprising, considering how much safer it was here for them. Sure, there were places a dragon could go to be treated like royalty, a few countries away and a few more just a jump across an ocean. Yet here, a dragon could live safely and freely— Britain outlawed the capturing of dragons, and as long as the dragons didn't cause trouble, they were allowed almost wherever they wished.

So perhaps sitting on million-year-old bones was not a good idea, but so long as she wasn't seen.... It wasn't like she was even heavy enough to leave a mark.

She glided out, feeling the need to stretch her wings, fly around a bit, see something other than dead things in various shapes and forms. She enjoyed staring down, watching the humans and their strange lives.

When suddenly something wet, smelly and sticky splattered into her. "Ack!" She growled in surprise, and went tumbling down out of the sky. The awful smell flooded her nostrils and made her nauseated, blurring her vision and tearing her eyes. She barely just managed to gain enough control over herself to catch the wind under her sticky wings to glide down and land on the edge of a rooftop.

"Ughhhh..." She growled, taking a few breaths, each one burning her throat from the smell.

She raised a wing to inspect it, and tried not to hurl up her insides at the sight of the splattering of yellowish greenish white on the usually beautiful Caribbean-blue membrane. She sighed and dropped her wing in disgust.

Bird droppings.

The odds, she mentally complained. *The odds!* Not an inch of her tiny body had been spared the barrage. She could almost feel the acid eating away at her shimmery, ocean-and-azure blue scales, feel it seeping into her obsidian black horns and talons and chestplates. Her ridged turquoise membraned spines that ran from her forehead down to her tail felt sticky when they flexed, and she wanted nothing more than to dive into a pond and wash away the scat. Though she had a feeling that the smell would stay with her a long while. Her silver eyes were still tearing from the pungent aroma.

She flung out her wings, hoping to whip away as much of it as she could so that she could at least fly to a pond. She was about to take off in search of said pond, when the sound of wheels and clattering metal distracted her.

She turned her snout down and looked at the alleyway. It was shaded by the overhanging roofs of the adjoining buildings and sported a door at the very end, so dark and camouflaged with the rest of the metal wall that she might not have noticed it had she not seen the cart rolling towards it.

Indeed, a man wearing shades and a pristine tuxedo was wheeling a trolley with a dark cloth atop it towards the door. The trolley was flanked by another man in suit and shades. Neither human spoke as they brought the rattling trolley to towards the door.

I should get out of here, she thought, getting an uneasy feeling from the men in suits. *And quickly,* she decided, spreading her wings to jump from the edge of the tile rooftop.

Yet when she was about to jump, her slimy talons slipped on the tile and she went falling down to the concrete below with a reptilian squawk of surprise. She clawed at the air, desperately tried to angle her wings, but in the end she hit the concrete with a *thump* and *crack.*

A bolt of pain seared through her left arm, but she bit back her cry of pain. Her heart thundered in her chest.

The clattering of the trolley halted. The man pushing the trolley turned around, and a blank face looked down at her. The thin lips curved upward just a slight. "Well, look what we have here. Think the boss'll pay extra if we bring in a surplus?" He commented to his companion, but his face remained intent on her.

No no no no no no no, she thought rapidly, struggling to her talons as the tall, thin man stalked towards her. Yet her left arm only collapsed beneath her— something was terribly wrong with it. She tried to flap her wings...

But by then, the man had reached her. "Most definitely," the other man replied. "And if she's pretty, she'll fetch even more."

Azara began desperately scrambling backwards, but the man easily covered the distance. She bared her teeth up at him, her face contorted into a snarl. *If I'm going down, I'm going down fighting!* She thought determinedly as she hissed up at the smirking man. "Leave me alone!" She growled, trying to look as intimidating as she could.

"Nah, she looks a bit worse for wear, but she has spirit. She rather looks like an angry kitten, doesn't she? People like kittens," the man above her replied, kneeling down to reach for her.

Kitten?! I am no kitten! But spirit, yes... I've got that. "And kittens have really sharp teeth!" She growled, snapping at the hand reaching towards her. *I will not go down without a fight!* She repeated.

But the hand clamped down around her in a movement so swift and practiced that she didn't have time to even nip him. She squirmed frustratedly in his firm grip.

"They like pretty kittens. She looks more like she's been sleeping in a dumpster for the last year." The man standing by the trolley said, though her view had been blocked so she recognized by voice. It sounded a lot closer now. "Smells like it too."

Well you try getting dropped on by a bird and you see how good you smell you—

"True, but that can be fixed," the man holding her said. A moment later, she felt herself being shoved into a barred box— a cage, she realized. She tried to lunge for the hand— to at least give him one good bite— but the hand was gone and the door was slammed closed before she could even take another breath.

She breathed furiously, and threw herself against the bars of her tiny cage for all the good it would do. "Ugh!" She growled, only causing a ripple of pain in her injured arm.

"Lass, it isn't going to help. It's solid and there's no way out." A voice said from the darkness around her— Irish, from the accent. "I've tried— trust me." He sounded so resigned, so defeated.

Azara tried to calm her furious breathing, still staring at the cloth behind the bars, not turning to face the voice. "Who are you? What happened? Who are these people?" She demanded.

"My name is Angus, and I'm here against my will just as you are. As for who these people are, that I suppose we are yet to find out," he answered.

Azara finally calmed her breathing. "Is there anyone else here?"

There was a pause before he replied. "I think you better see for yourself, lass," he said finally.

From the tone of his voice, it wasn't good, so she braced herself, and turned around.

And before her, were dozens upon dozens of stacked, individual, caged dragons.

5

Into the Unknown

Isis listened drowsily to the two conversing dragons, awakened by a foul stench invading her nose. She decided to stay awake upon realizing that gone was the sound of rumbling engines. For good or ill, they were no longer in some human vehicle. She had lost track of the hours she had spent inside her cage as it was transferred from cars into crates into trucks and to places that must have been very, very high up as her ears had popped in adjustment to altitude. Wherever she was now, she had a feeling it was a long way from Egypt.

It was also much, much colder, and she felt chilled to the bone— she was used to the warm sun and sands of the desert. "What... What do they want with all of us? And where are we being taken?" The new voice asked.

Isis had been asking herself the same questions for as long as she had been in this cage. "I don't know," she answered. There must be some reason. *Why would humans just randomly decide to start mass-capturing dragons?* She thought. *It can't just be out of pure human cruelty.* In that she was determined— humans were many things, cruel, unkind, but she knew that there was also good in them, and they wouldn't spontaneously do something like this just for pleasure. "Where are you all from?" She suddenly asked into the dark.

She waited a few moments, then some dragons answered. "Ireland," a male voice volunteered.

"Siberia," a meek voice offered.

Then came the barrage of answers. France, Romania, Switzerland, Sweden, Israel, Spain, Ethiopia, Norway, China, even one from as far away as New York. Finally a last voice chimed in— the newest voice. "Britain. London, when I was captured."

"So we're in London now," She thought aloud. *At least I know where we are for now. Yet these dragons were brought from all over the world...* Her brow furrowed. *But why?*

A weak voice then asked through the darkness. "Isis...?"

Isis perked her ears at the sound of her name and craned her neck, looking for the familiar source of the sound. Her eyes then locked on the silver scales of a dragon a few cages away. "Iah! Iah, oh no... They caught you too..."

Iah nodded her head. The Goddess of the Moon looked unusually subdued, and Isis realized that something looked terribly wrong with the angle of Iah's wing. "They snatched me right out of my temple, just after the priests had gone," she explained.

Isis nodded slowly. "I was caught right after the priests had left as well, but at my grandmother's obelisk...." Suddenly a new theory popped into her head. "Did anyone here have any rank, any form of importance? Does anyone here have some form of occupation?" She asked.

Just as they had with the locations, a slow thread of answers eventually turned into a cascade.

"I lived in a museum."

"I pretended to be a creature of myth..."

"I... I tended fires..."

Baker, thief, painter, hunter, spy, pet, commander, companion, scientist, librarian, chieftain, pirate... *It doesn't add up.*

Isis was cut from her thoughts by the sound of metal doors sliding open, and the clattering of the trolley finally coming to a stop. Isis wearily looked around, as did several of the other dragons. Most of the time, when whatever transport they were on stopped, it only meant transfer to another form of transport.

A moment later, the cloth was whipped from the stacks of cages. Bright lights glared down at them, and Isis blinked at the sudden brightness. She tried to look around...

Everything was so blurry... But she could make out that they were in a room. A small, metal room with doors on both ends.

"Fresh set. Shouldn't be too ruffled, just as you requested. Most of the injuries shouldn't be too hard for you to mend," a tall, slim man said.

"I told you no injuries. They are supposed to be ready for inspection in just a few days," an annoyed, male voice said.

Then a newer voice chimed in— it was one that she had heard a few times before, but only in the past few days. "Oh come now! Their bones have got to be *this* tiny. How long could it take for them to heal?" A feminine voice complained, accented by footsteps as a blurry figure sauntered around the room. Isis was still acclimating to the light, so everything looked like vague figures.

"Just go," the annoyed male voice commanded. "You've all done enough harm in one day. I will be reporting this to the boss."

Isis studied the man who had just spoken as best she could. He was broad and wore a white coat, had very little hair, and was currently pulling plastic gloves over his hands.

"Alright, alright, report our disobedience to the *boss*. It's not like they'll *do anything*, sitting in that *room* all day—"

"We should go," The slim man then interrupted. Isis was able to see enough to watch as he gave her a stern glare.

The woman glared at him in return, but stalked out the door, swiftly followed by the man.

The man in a white coat then turned to the stacks of cages, and Isis stared right back at him. He scanned over the cages before sauntering over, and selecting a cage from the corner of the box-shaped stack. It contained a yellow-and-blue dragon with black horns and chestplates, and, Isis noted, a broken arm.

Despite her injury the little dragon hissed and snarled at the human as he carried her over to a metal table nearby. All the remaining caged dragons tensely watched, and Isis could smell their fear.

That scent set off something in her mind, something that was engraved from years of leading civilizations. The urge to protect, to help her people.

She was miles away from Egypt, but now, these dragons had become her people.

She watched intently as the man opened the cage and snatched the dragon inside firmly within his hand with a practiced grip. No matter how much the blue dragon struggled, he held her tight in his fist as he inspected her.

"Well, someone looks like they could do with a wash," the man murmured, then walked her over to a sink in a wall.

Isis wanted to look away as the poor dragon was rinsed off and given a painful looking scrubbing until her azure and ocean blue scales shined, all trace of the yellow now gone. The dragon never stopped fighting the entire time.

The human then brought her back over to the table and inspected her arm. "That's going to need mending," he said to himself, and set the dragon back in her cage— though he didn't bother closing the door. "Now don't bother leaving, or you're going to get to take a long nap for the rest of the day," the man warned.

There has to be a way to get us out of here... She thought as the human then returned to the stack of dragons and removed the cage to her left, containing a green dragon with golden horns and chestplates. This dragon growled at the human, but put up less of a fight as he was inspected, then returned to his cage placed beside the blue dragon's.

The human came for her next. She slid on the smooth metal floor of her cage as she was lifted up and carried over to the table. A moment later the cage door was open, and there was a hand reaching in for her.

Be brave. Be calm. You must save your people, she told herself, refusing to succumb to fear as firm, cold hands wrapped around her.

She was held up before him as he looked over her. "So much jewelry for such a little creature. You won't be needing that anymore," he said to himself, and set her down on the table, one hand still firmly clamped around her to keep her from flying away.

That was when she noticed it— a little button on the wall next to one of the sets of metal doors. It was red, with little white lettering beneath it...

The man began removing her jewelry, her necklaces and rings... And she began to pretend to be very, *very* upset. "Hey!" She roared. "That is *ancient Egyptian gold!* Get your *human hands off it*! *Now!* Before I summon the *powers* of the *sun* down upon you!" She growled, growing increasingly feisty. "That was my *great grandmother's horn ring*, you will *give it back right now*!"

Meanwhile, the man seemed to only look annoyed, fumbling about her to take her copious expensive things from her. When he tried to take a fancy, platinum anklet off her, she clutched it persistently with her hind talons. "*Hey!* This is *mine*!" She roared... while she slowly, slyly slipped off a jeweled, solid gold bracelet from her own wrist.

The man easily wrenched the anklet from her, yet she had already gotten her bracelet in her tiny talons.

And before he could even see what she was doing, she had it sailing through the air.

And it crashed into the little red button.

"*NOOO!* You *stupid* dragon!" The man roared as red light filled the room and a siren began to blare. He dropped her to lunge for the button, just as the opposite door was opened by a tuxedoed man, his mouth already opened in question.

She realized in a heartbeat that there was no way she could get all of the dragons out of their cages in time... So she turned to the two dragons who had been left with their cages open. "You two, run, now!" She commanded.

They stared back at her for a fraction of a second, then darted to their talons. "You must get to the Dragon Queen— only she can help us now. It is up to you now! Now fly!"

And so they bolted in the blur of blue and green for the door, past the confused and frustrated looking man at the door. Not a second later, the man in the white coat had reached the button and depressed it again, turning off the blaring siren and the bright red lights. "What is going on?!" The tuxedoed man asked angrily.

Isis stared at him. No, not at him, at the area *past* him. Towards where the blue and green dragons had bolted. For a moment, she was tempted to leap into the sky after them, to freedom...

But then she looked at the caged dragons that still remained. *I cannot abandon them.* She decided, and glanced once more at the open door. *Whoever you are, dragon of blue and dragon of green, our lives are in your talons.*

And she was not afraid when a gloved hand closed around her.

And she glared with all her heart at the coated man, even as she felt a sharp sting in her thigh.

Even as she felt her consciousness drain out of her, and she descended into darkness.

6
Escape

Angus was beating his wings with every ounce of energy he had.

He followed the blue dragon through the winding metal corridors, neither of them knowing the way out. They all looked the same... Gray metal, the occasional windowless door with a number label that they could make no sense of... He may have been a dragon who posed as a legend, but he knew little about how to escape from a labyrinth.

They were running out of time— it would be a matter of seconds till the man in the white coat told the others of their escape. The thought of being chased by the people in dark suits again sent a surge of adrenaline through him, and he flapped his wings even harder. "Lass," he called to the blue dragoness. "Any idea how to get out of here?"

"Not a clue," the dragoness replied.

Well then, Angus mentally muttered, when suddenly a door flung open in front of them. *Nonononononono*— both Angus and the blue dragon tried to slow down from their rapid flight but they were going far too fast—

Splat.

They crashed into the door. Angus had at least managed to turn slightly so the brunt of the impact went to his shoulder rather than his snout, but his head still thwacked against the door hard enough for him to see stars. He fell to the cold metal ground, feeling quite like a swatted fly.

"Aha! Perfect!" A man exclaimed, and a moment later Angus felt human hands scooping him up.

Ughhhh... No.... Angus groggily groaned in his head. *Not again... I can't be captured again... We need to find... Find the Queen...* But the man's grip was firm on his little body, and the blue dragon in the man's other hand looked as if she had been knocked clean out cold.

Angus let himself be carried by the man, who was wearing a simple blue shirt and tan trousers rather than a dark suit. *Did we escape...? Is this just a human from the outside?* He wondered.

His heart sank as he was shoved into a cage, only slightly larger than the one in which he had been confined to for who knew how many days. He was joined by Azara a few seconds later, and with a metallic clang their door was shut.

He was in a cage. Again.

He felt like he wanted to explode. Like he wanted to just fall and sleep and never wake up. It amazed him how one could be so close to freedom, only for it to just get... Snatched away in the blink of an eye. Or, in retrospect, the swing of a door.

He dejectedly watched through the bars of the cage as it was carried down a corridor, waiting to emerge into the room of that terrible man with a white coat, to be punished for escaping...

The blue-shirted man carrying them pushed open a metal door, and what was revealed was not the coated man's room with it's cold table and sink and two sets of doors. Not in the slightest.

Instead, a spacious rectangular room spread out before his eyes. There was a counter with a cash register by the door they had just come through. Angus looked around for other details, any means of escape, and his gaze wandered to the walls.

The walls.

Every inch of them was lined with cages. Countless, variety-sized cages of Pocket Dragons. Some were small, individual cages, others were far larger containing little habitats of dragons, all pitifully fake looking. Plastic leaves adorned a large glass birdcage full of dreary looking green dragons, and clay shells dotted a habitat of blue dragons. A habitat with a wallpaper of a crackling fire contained some very dejected looking red dragons, and a background of stars nearly camouflaged a collection of dark colored dragons.

Yet there was one thing that Angus noticed above all. Above all the colorful cages and mock biome recreations.

The hopelessness.

He could see it in every dragon's eyes.

The weary, sad, utter lack of hope for their survival, for their lives, of ever escaping this place. They all looked like the world could end tomorrow, and they wouldn't care. For them, the world had already ended, long ago.

"Here you are!" The man carrying them announced. It was then that Angus noticed the old man in tan trousers and a white shirt waiting by one of the walls of dragons, frowning at the habitats. "Two beautiful dragons, perfectly healthy I assure you."

The old man turned, revealing a white beard, white hair, and striking blue eyes. "I really should report this place. The health of these dragons is terrible!" Were the first words he uttered.

"No no sir, these dragons are all perfectly healthy! Their scales are just a bit dull, that's all. But here I've got a very vibrant pair, just for you!" The man carrying them insisted, holding up the cage for emphasis. This new height brought them eye-to-eye with the old man.

The old man stepped over to them and peered inside the cage, his eyes glazing over them, studying them. Beside him, the blue dragoness was still unconscious, and all Angus could think to do was stare back at the man. "Are you sure the blue one is alright? She's pretty, but she doesn't look quite right."

"Oh yes, just fine sir!" The blue shirted man assured. "She's just taking a nap. Dragons are really quite like cats— they like to spend the majority of their time sleeping."

"Hmmm..." The old man fingered his beard, studying them in the cage again. "Well at least they look cleaner than the others. Such magnificent eyes on the green one... They'll have to do," he concluded.

The man holding them sounded ecstatic. "Fantastic! Just come with me and I'll ring you up..."

Angus clutched the bars of the cage to hold on as it was swiftly brought over to the counter with a cash register and set down. *We're going to be... Bought...* He realized with disgust. *Like... Like fish! Or hamsters! Or parakeets!* Angus didn't know Britain very well, but he did know that dragon pet stores like this were illegal— selling dragons was a black market, something that was unfortunately common. Despite how common dragons were, the human's ridiculous desire to own them and barbarous belief in the magical properties of their assorted body parts made dragons fetch a high price in many parts of the world, especially places where they were illegal. *The outrage!* Yet there was nothing he could do...

But watch.

And Angus watched as the old man handed several hundred-pound bills to the blue-shirted man.

"Good day sir, enjoy your dragons," the pet store owner said.

Angus remembered to clutch the bars again as the old man lifted up the cage and began stalking towards the door. "If this wasn't the only place in all of Great Britain to buy a dragon, I would be reporting this place to the police." The old man said by way of goodbye, before he pushed open the metal door that led to the outside world.

Waiting just outside was an old blue truck, into which the old man climbed. Settling into the drivers seat, he held the cage to his eyes again. Angus stared blankly back at him. "Yes... I do believe my grandson shall like you two," the man murmured to himself before setting the cage down in the passenger seat.

The car growled into life, and Angus went sliding back in the cage as the vehicle made a sudden lurch forward. *We failed,* was all Angus could think of as the car settled into a steady drive. He looked up out the window to see to his dismay as the tall buildings of London slowly gave way to open sky. They must be leaving the city. *We failed.*

He thought of the amber-golden dragon, her words echoing in his head. *"You must find the Dragon Queen. Only she can help you now."*

He shook his head in despair. *I'm sorry,* he thought, and he wished that the golden dragon could hear him.

Hear him as London and all the trapped dragons disappeared far behind them.

For he had no idea how they would find the Dragon Queen now.

7

The Glass Cage

Frida huddled in the farthest back corner of her open cage, as far away from the man in the white coat as she could get. After the man had returned the unconscious golden dragon to her cage, the man had come for Frida.

Out of pure terror, she didn't so much as struggle as the man inspected her, turning her over in his freezing cold gloved hands. She just let herself hang limp, and she squeezed her eyes shut for the majority of it until she felt herself returned to the hard steel of her cage, into which she had gladly retreated.

Occasionally she glanced at the golden dragon out cold in her cage. *She was so brave...* She thought. *I wish I were brave...* She wished that she could have helped save the dragons, helped others escape. She wished she could have been so clever as to distract the man with cold hands, to notice the button on the wall. *For while she was surely plotting a way to save us, I was wishing I could disappear...* She thought ashamedly.

The only thing she could think to do know was count the cages. Forty-eight dragons had been inspected so far, not including the lucky two that had escaped. Fifty-one cages remained. Some dragons, such as herself, had been placed in their cages and put on one side of the table. Several others, about a dozen so far, had been placed on a metal dolly in the corner of the room. She wondered why some dragons were being separated, but she couldn't figure it out. She glanced again at the golden dragon. *I bet she would be able to figure it out...*

Suddenly, a man in a suit opened the door she was closest too. "Are they ready?" The man asked, sounding impatient.

The man in the white coat continued inspecting the purple dragon he was holding. "No," he answered simply. "I've got another hour, so leave me to my work. Unless you want it to take two hours to get through them all."

The man in the suit looked increasingly upset. "Times up, Doctor. Our guest has arrived earlier than anticipated. We need these dragons ready *now*."

The Doctor set the dragon inside their cage. "Is this a ruse to get me done quicker or are they *actually* here?" He asked, placing his hands in the table squarely.

"This is no joke, Doctor." The suited man stormed in. "We need these dragons in the habitat in fifteen minutes."

The Doctor still didn't budge. "Well, I'm afraid that's impossible. I've got thirty-six dragons that are acceptable to be taken. I'm not a miracle worker. Your just going to have to get me more time, or make do with thirty six dragons."

The man in the suit looked flustered for a moment. "Fine," he finally said. "But next time, I need the dragons done early. We can't have this happening again."

The Doctor sauntered over to a wall where a blue button lay embedded. "Next time," the Doctor said. "Get me the dragons on time." He said, and pushed the button.

Frida heard the sound of metal gears whirring behind her, in the direction of her open cage door. She slowly turned around, her eyes wide...

As a large, circular hole opened up behind them, glowing with a neon blue light from within.

And not a moment later, she was sucked right into it.

The strong, sucking winds pulled her inside, right out of her cage, and into the tunnel. The neon lights inside blinded her, and her only senses consisted of the feeling of the wind blasting and blowing around her and her occasional slamming against the metal walls. She had the vague sense of going up, then forward.... She caught glimpses of other dragons also being tossed and turned and thrown about in the tunnel. But she had the sense that they were all being blown in the same direction.

Then suddenly, they were plummeted downward, and the harsh neon light was replaced by daylight as the tunnel disappeared around them and wide open space took its place.

"Ugh!" Frida exclaimed when she hit the hard, dirt ground. She felt several more similar sounds around her as the other dragons struck the ground.

Slowly, Frida lifted her snout from the dirt, her head ringing from the tunnel. *I guess now I know why the cage doors were left open...* She mentally groaned. *I wish I had been able to figure that out earlier...* She sighed, then finally lifted her head to survey where she was now.

Fear closed around her like darkness after a candle was snuffed out.

For she was right in the middle of a massive, glass cage.

The other dragons around her surveyed the area, and she did the same. Trees and plants surrounded them, and a mock daylight rained down on them from lights in the blue-metal ceiling. A crisp blue pool of water welled in the very center of the grassy clearing into which they had all been deposited, and several dragons were now crawling their way onto the bank. The cage was truly gigantic— it could have probably housed hundreds if not thousands of pocket dragons. The whole design was circular, and she realized that their enclosure was indeed a massive, hollow cylinder. It was like a fish tank... And she was on the inside.

She, and the other dragons, were the fish.

Frida narrowed her eyes, looking past the glass that circled around them, and noticed that surrounding the entirety of the massive cylinder was another room with walls and floors of black metal.

Not just a fish tank.

An observation room.

And then she noticed the man standing in the outside room. He also wore the black suit and shades, yet he was quite broad and somewhat heavy compared to the other humans she had seen here. He stood with his hands behind his back in an alert posture. "Attention, dragons!" He commanded.

At least, Frida *thought* he said. His mouth moved, but the actual voice came from above them. She glanced up to notice several sets of tiny holes in the ceiling, and she wondered if they were somehow the source of the sound. Meanwhile, at the sound of the voice, most of the dragons scattered to the assorted trees.

Frida was about to spread her wings and join them, when she glanced to the side and saw the golden dragon, still lying unconscious in the dirt. She glanced between the dragons hiding in the trees and the golden dragon...

She lunged for the golden dragon. Yet just as she reached her, the voice from above boomed again: "I am The Keeper, and you are what I'm keeping," the man introduced. "Welcome to The Habitat, your new home."

The Habitat, his words rang in her ears. *No... This is not a habitat. No matter how much they try to deceive us... This is a cage. A Glass Cage...*

"I need to lay out some rules, dragons, and if anyone, anyone, disobeys them, you will all be punished." Frida stood by the unconscious dragoness, too terrified to move. She wanted to pick up the dragoness, carry her into the trees... But her talons felt as if they had turned to stone. The Keeper continued. "Firstly, you must all be on your best behavior whenever we have guests," the Keeper warned. "No talking, no trying to escape, nothing out of ordinary animal behavior." Frida wished that she could disappear into the ground. "You will all be fed and watered and taken care of. It's very simple— you behave, and we'll take care of you." The Keeper paused for emphasis. "Fail to behave... And our part of the bargain is nullified." Ice crept along Frida's spine. The

Keeper then turned around and sauntered towards a metal door behind him. "And now, it is time to behave, dragons, for we have a very important guest..." The Keeper depressed a button by the door with a pudgy finger. "We are ready for you, sir," he spoke into a series of holes above the button.

And Frida felt the entire population of the Glass Cage hold its breath, could hear the heartbeat of every dragon, as the metal doors slid open.

8
Snow and Storms

Kostya leaned back in his chair, the end of his pen held to his chin as he thought. A handwritten book sat in his lap, open to the last page. *It just needs one last sentence...*

Something nice... He thought, twiddling the pencil.

He cast his gaze towards the fire which crackled in its hearth, filling the room with a comforting heat and warm glow. It almost seemed to dance as if it had a mind of its own.

It might, he thought amusedly. *After all, it*

is dear Frida's fire. Her fire has always seemed special...

Just then the words he needed flashed into his mind, and with a growing grin he planted his pen to the last page and elegantly drew the last letters of his story. He carefully set down his pen on the table beside him and took a moment to reread that final sentence a few time over. *Yes... It's perfect,* he decided.

Gently closing the book and picking it up in his hands, he scrambled to his feet with an energy he rarely experienced so late in his years, and hobbled to the door. He fiddled with the handle and threw open the door excitedly, not bothering to close it as he joyously tramped out into the snow.

"Frida!" He called, looking around for her. "Frida!" He scanned the fencepost where she often liked to sit and watch the world go by, but didn't see her there. Turning, he ambled down towards the center of the village where a massive fire burned to keep the area safe and warm. *Maybe she's stoking the fires,* he suspected. *She usually does that in the mornings, but...* He reached the bonfire, but didn't see the little ice dragon anywhere by it.

He furrowed his brows and hugged the book to his side with one arm. *Where could she be?* He scanned around the ring of little cabins, and his eyes landed on the woodcarver's house. Frida often liked to watch the carver at work. *Maybe she decided to watch him today,* he hoped.

Snow crunching underfoot, he approached the woodcarver's elaborate door, raised his thin-skinned hand, and knocked. A few moments later, the door creaked and slid open, revealing the tall, hearty, brown-haired man inside. There was a carving tool still in his hand, and he wore a brown coat despite being inside. "My friend," Kostya spoke quickly in the local language, "May I come in?"

The woodcarver looked curious but nodded, stepping back and gesturing for him to enter. "What is the matter?" Asked the carver.

Kostya stepped inside and waited till the carver had closed the door to answer, too concerned to waste a moment surveying the menagerie of elaborate carvings that decorated the small, otherwise simple house. "My Frida, is she here with you? Have you seen her today?" He asked.

The woodcarver raised his thick brows. "No, I have not seen her today," he answered. "Is she missing?"

Kostya frowned. "I'm not sure. She isn't where she usually is this time of day."

The carver fiddled with the tool in his hand. "Maybe she decided to do something else today. She's a dragon— they aren't always predictable. She would usually be with you by night, correct? Maybe you should just go back home and wait for her," he pointed out. "She is small. There are any number of places she could be. You would be wiser to wait."

The old man shook his head. "No, no Frida is not like that," he insisted, more to himself than to the carver. "She keeps to her routine. And I called to her — she would never ignore a call."

The woodcarver scratched the back of his head with his free hand. "Then what are you planning to do?"

Kostya tightened his lip into a thin line in thought. Finally, he answered. "Take a final look around the village— check at the houses. Sometimes she likes the artist's house. I'm going back to my house to prepare," he instructed.

The carver set his tool down on a nearby elaborate table. "Very well, sir. But what are you preparing for?"

The old man was already escorting himself out of the house. "I'm going to the woods. She doesn't like them but it's the only other place she could have gone."

The carver beat him to the door and opened it for him, grabbing a hat from a rack as he did. "Alright. But still Kostya, why do you worry so much? She's probably fine, just taking a nap somewhere."

"How many coats do you have, my friend?" Kostya asked spontaneously.

"I beg your pardon sir?" The woodcarver sounded confused.

"How many coats do you have?" Kostya repeated.

The carver glanced down at his own brown coat. "Three, I think, somewhere."

Kostya began tramping out into the snow. "Well, if we can't find Frida before her fires extinguish, then you'll be wanting to find them and be layering up. It's going to get chilly."

With that he ambled back to his house. Rapidly he threw on his coat and gathered up the necessities in a pack, including a pencil sketch of Frida that the village's artist had drawn, as well as any other supplies he might need.

He paused by the door, taking one final glance over the cabin, making sure that he hadn't forgotten anything... And quite possibly wishing that Frida would pop around the corner, saying that she had merely nodded off in the back... *No. I saw her leave this morning. And she would always greet me when she comes back...*

He turned and opened the door.

The woodcarver waited for him outside. Kostya hobbled through his doorway and closed the door, digging through his jacket pocket for the keys. "I presume the lack of my Frida's presence means that you did not find her?" He assumed as he fiddled with the keys and locked his door.

The carver shook his head. "I'm afraid not. No one has seen her since this morning. I went by every house."

Kostya's heart sank. He had been mostly sure that something was wrong, though still he'd had a flicker of hope... He turned away and began to march off towards the woods. "If I do not return by dusk..." He started, but didn't bother to finish his sentence.

Leaving the village behind, he ambled through into the woods, tramping through the snow with his snowshoes, looking for those beautiful blue scales, those stunning dual colored eyes. He carefully checked the hunter's traps, concerned that she might have gotten herself caught in one of them.

It's so silent... He thought absentmindedly. *No wolf howls... No birds... No rabbits... Nothing.*

Gleaming metal caught his eye, and he worked his way over to it. Partially hidden beneath snow lay a metal cage trap, the trap activated. He eagerly bent over, pawing for the catch to open it. "Frida?"

He released the trap, and waited, hopeful to see her little scaly body come zipping out—

With a fluffy blur, a snow hare raced out of the trap. Its fluffy white tail disappeared into the woods within a heartbeat.

Kostya sighed. *Where are you, Frida?* Suddenly, he heard a mechanical whirring sound in the air. It grew louder and louder—until he could see the sleek black body of a helicopter flying past. He stared up at it with wide eyes. "No..."

The helicopter flew past him, back in the direction of the village. By a sudden instinct he started chasing after it-— snow flying behind him as he raced. He soon lost sight of it, but still he could hear the mechanical whirring of the chopper.

He broke through the treeline and sprinted back towards the village, his eyes flicking between the ground and helicopter that continued sailing through the air away from him.

He slowed to an exhausted halt next to a rather surprised woodcarver and caught his breath. "My friend, grab an axe and begin chopping. You're going to need wood to keep the village warm," he panted.

"Why Kostya? What is it? Did you not find Frida?" The carver asked.

Kostya took another deep breath of the cold air and began trotting again.

"Where are you going, Kostya?" Called the carver.

Kostya bellowed back to him despite his exhaustion, but never stopped running. "I'm going to the city. I'm going to find my Frida!"

Alastair Alby swiveled back and forth a couple times in his swivel chair, tired of typing and deleting and typing and deleting over and over again. His laptop lay on the wooden desk in front of him, unfinished virtual documents awaiting him. His private director's office was lavishly furnished, and he kept glancing at the pictures on the black marble wall— mostly of his sheep— the overfilled bookcases behind him, and the flatscreen television mounted on the wall to provide a live video of the tourists visiting the natural wonder below.

Of course, he could always just look at the floor to ceiling window to his left that overlooked the entirety of the Giant's Causeway itself; the wonder of hundreds of natural hexagonal stones.

That window currently occupied the majority of his attention. There had been a terrible tempest earlier that morning, but the storm had since stopped, and he was most concerned by the lack of a certain routine visitor.

Every morning a golden and green dragon would fly past that very window, coming in to do his day’s work of messing with the tourists and, presumably, stealing what he could from the cafe. Yet Alastair had long since decided that the former easily made up for the latter of the dragon's activities. *We are remarkably lucky,* he thought, *to have a dragon who looks just like the one from the legend of the Giants Causeway come visit every day of his own accord. The tourists he brings in...*

He frowned, furrowing his brow at the window. *So the question is, where is the little dragon today*? This worry had been gnawing at him since that morning. *He didn't fly past today...*

He had never, of course, ever spoken to the dragon. Nor did he expect the dragon to know him whatsoever. Yet still, simply by observing him, he felt as if he had developed an understanding of the way the little creature lived.

He glanced back at the laptop, the screen having gone black from disuse, letting his aged reflection stare back at him. He straightened an unruly lapel of his gray business coat. "Gilroy!" Alastair called.

A few moments later his wooden door opened, revealing a skinny young redheaded man wearing a sweater and vest. "Yes Mr. Alby?" He asked.

Alby tried not to look concerned. "Gilroy, let me know if you hear any sightings of our dragon today. Anything at all," he said casually.

"Yes sir," Gilroy said, looked about to turn away, then paused and asked: "Is there something wrong, Mr. Alby?"

Alastair sighed almost inaudibly. "I certainly hope not, Gilroy," he answered. "Oh, and get me some coffee, would you?"

"Yes sir," his assistant said, and the boy left and closed the door.

Alastair looked over to the window again, looking at the gloomy clouds over the gray hexagonal stones.

Then tapped on his laptop and returned to work.

9
Welcome to Willough

Azara woke as she was suddenly jostled inside her cage.

Wait.... Inside a cage?! She suddenly realized as she felt metal beneath her claws.

Another bump shook the cage, and she drowsily lifted her head. *No... There shouldn't be bars... We were escaping...* She mentally groaned. *Why are there bars...*

The green dragon who she had been escaping with was laying nearby, curled up like a cat with his tail over his snout. His bright golden eyes were open, however, and he lifted his own head at noticing she was awake.

"Welcome back, lass," he said dejectedly.

Azara groaned aloud this time. "Would you *please* stop calling me that."

The green dragon lowered his head, his ears flicked down in an apologetic position. "Sorry, la-miss?" He shook his head, then looked at her in silent question.

Azara half sighed, half rolled her eyes. "Azara."

The green dragon nodded. "I'm Angus."

Azara flexed her wings in the little cage. It had plenty of room for them to both to have done so without touching wings, but it was nevertheless a cage. "So what happened?" She demanded. "We were escaping, and I don't remember anything past... A door." She recalled. "Where are we now? Where are we going?" For she could tell that they were going *somewhere,* based on the rattling and jostling of their cage.

Angus shifted into a proper sitting position. "Well, after we flew into the door, we were caught. Except, not by one of the people we've seen so far— and we were taken into a pet store...." He looked down at his talons, then nodded towards the space behind him, where Azara realized a man was sitting, driving the vehicle that carried them. "We were bought. I don't know where we are going now, or where we are. All I know is that we're not in London anymore."

Azara tried to rise to her talons, but then hissed at the pain in her arm. She had almost forgotten her injury, and now the pain blazed through her arm in sharp reminder. She pushed herself to her talons again, this time only using three of her legs, and limped to the edge of the cage, then peered up, trying to see if she could spot any landmarks from the window despite the odd angle.

But she saw no landmarks, or any building of any sort. In fact, she saw *trees*. Trees arching gracefully over whatever road they were on. Trees so dense it looked as if they were driving right through a forest.

Then, suddenly, the trees were gone. The truck made a sudden halt, and Azara felt herself be thrown right into the bars of the cage. "AGGHK!" She roared in pain as her bad arm crashed against the metal, and blackness crept across her vision. *No,* she thought determinedly. *I'm not going unconscious again. Not now.*

A moment later, she felt the cage being heaved up, and she clutched a bar with her good arm in order to not slide around. She watched as they were lifted up, and she surveyed their new location.

They were, in what appeared to be, a village. A scattering of houses dotted the area before them, many of them made of logs or stone or bricks— as if built a couple hundred years ago. The roads were paved with cobblestone, wide enough for cars or horses, though neither currently occupied the streets. Azara knew what sort of village this was. She had heard of them before, read about them in museum books. Small little sanctuaries where people chose to live simpler lives— rejecting most forms of modernity, yet accepting what was necessary to make life easier, such as cars and electricity for light.

The rest of life was usually augmented by the help of pocket dragons.

However, there were hundreds of different cultures that lived like this, and it was impossible to know which one by first impression.

Meanwhile, Azara could feel every swing of the little cage in her bad arm. She still didn't know exactly what was wrong with it, though she suspected it was broken— she knew nothing else that could cause this much pain.

She kept her jaw clenched as she grimly watched their surroundings go by.

It was a small village, with only about a couple dozen houses. There was a large village square that she noticed, which looked large enough to accommodate all the residents of a village this size. A simple fountain made up the center of the square, as well as a round stone dais with a simple stone table in the center. The square looked as if it was being prepared for festivities— flowers gilded the base of the stone table, and tables were being set up around the square.

They made a turn down a path leading away from the square, cutting it from her view and replacing it with that of a house.

It was a simple two-storied house with a wooden shed attached, and from the looks of it, was connected to electricity, as she noticed several rooms were lit with artificial light.

The old man brought them up to the porch, then opened the creaky door. Azara craned her neck to see inside...

Only for her view to suddenly be cast black as some sort of cloth was thrown over their cage. "Blast!" Azara exclaimed. *Now how am I supposed to see all the exits and windows to plan our escape...* She mentally growled.

"Grandfather, was that you?" The voice of a boy called. It sounded young— around twelve, Azara estimated.

"Yes, it's me. The door's being creaky again. I'll have to fix it," the old man answered. Azara listened intently, eager to glean any useful information that she could potentially use to escape.

"Where did you go?" The boy asked. "I didn't see you leave."

"Just had to run some errands," the elderly man answered. "Now I'm going up to bed— I want to get an early start for tomorrow." The tone of his voice implied that something potentially very special was going on tomorrow.

Azara wondered if it had anything to do with the decorations being set up in the town square. The steady but slowed sound of footsteps on creaky wood gave Azara the impression that they were going upstairs. *Ack, I wish I could see!* She mentally complained again.

A few seconds later, Azara heard the sound of another door being opened, and then the feeling that their cage was being set down. The old man then lifted up the cloth to peek in at them with his piercing blue eyes.

Azara didn't even look at him. She looked everywhere else— it would appear that they were in some sort of closet, judging by the clothes hanging beneath them. Behind the elderly man's face she could see what appeared to be a bedroom— with several windows, she noted.

The man's speaking drew her attention back to his face. "You two almost got me discovered back there!" He said in reprimand, but from the crinkling of his eyes she could tell he wasn't truly upset. "I need you to be quiet now— don't want to spoil the surprise!" He said with a wink. "Oh, and— welcome to Willough." With that, he dropped the cloth back over their cage, and with a creak, Azara assumed the closet door was closed.

Instantly, she turned to the dark figure that was Angus. "We need to get out of here."

Angus sighed. "I know. But how? We're in a cage, in a closet, in a house, in a village who knows how far away from London."

If Azara's arm hadn't been injured, she would have been pacing. "There has to be some way to get out of here. If we could only get out of this cage..." Her mind raced as she tried to think of how to get out.

"Even if we *did* get out, how far could you go with that arm? I know you can fly, but the pain—" Angus tried to persuade.

"— Is irrelevant." Azara deflected. "Once I get out, I can find a healer, then I can be a nice, long way away from those snatchers." *I wonder if we could burn through these bars...* She considered as she spoke. It was unlikely— if the cage was designed for trapping dragons as it surely was, it would be made of metal that wouldn't burn even under the intensity of dragonflame.

"But..." Angus sounded confused. "We need to find the queen. The golden dragon that helped us escape told us to—"

"Yes, I know." Azara interrupted him again. "And I know she sacrificed herself to save us... But Angus, is there really anything that even the queen could do to help? Stuff like this has happened for thousands of years... We were rarely able to stop it then, what difference would it make now? We should be glad we escaped and be smart, and stay as far away from those snatchers as we can get." She sighed. Angus looked as if he was about to say something, but Azara interrupted him once more. "But before anything, we need to get out of this cage," she insisted. "Do you have any abilities that might help?" She asked.

There was a longer silence than she expected. "I don't have any abilities," he finally answered.

Azara felt herself slow down just a bit, and she raised a brow. "Really? That's... Rare." She murmured. "Not even firebreath?" She could see him shake his head in a 'no' through the dark. She had never met a powerless dragon before... Usually a dragon at least had firebreath, sometimes another ability that was passed down in a family. Complete lack of any magical spark whatsoever was a genetic anomaly that only occurred every one in ten thousand dragons or so. *Of course,* she mentally complained. *The golden dragon was seriously out of luck that the two who she saved happened to be us— a dragon without magic and then me.*

"Do you have anything that could help us?" Angus asked.

Azara slowly shook her head. "Nothing that would help," she replied. For no, her type of magic would not help her here.

She could see Angus rest his head in his talons. "Then I suppose all we can do is wait," he murmured.

Azara waited a moment, then lowered herself down to the metal cage floor and curled up. "Yes, I suppose so..." She agreed.

Azara awoke to darkness and the sound of creaky wood— the familiar sound of an opening door. A moment later, the cloth was lifted from their cage so that the elderly man could peer inside. "It's the day!" The man excitedly whispered. "It's time to get you to your places," he said, and dropped the cloth again.

Not a second after they were plunged back into darkness did Azara feel that the cage was being lifted. Beside her Angus had lifted his head, so she knew that he was awake.

"Where are we going?" He drowsily whispered.

Azara tightly held a bar with her good arm, trying to keep herself steady. "I don't know," she replied. "Though I have a feeling we're going to find out," she murmured, half to herself.

After the creaking of a swinging door, the darkness inside their cage reduced just a slight. *We must be outside now, in the daytime,* she realized. Their cage was carried for a little while longer before the cloth was finally removed.

Alas, Azara only got a meager glance of the town square before a hand grabbed around her, and she bit back on her growl of pain at her arm being squeezed. The pain disoriented her so much that she had little energy to struggle.

Azara saw stone walls rise around her— a box. She and Angus were being placed inside a box. Finally the hand released them, and Azara took several gasping breaths as the pain in her arm slowly dissipated. Yet before she could get up, to bolt into the sky...

A stone lid was placed atop the box, casting them once more into darkness.

"No!" She roared. *I shouldn't have let my pain distract me, I should have fought, should have escaped... Now I'm just in another box! Another cage*! She was getting very, *very* tired of cages. She climbed to her talons and launched herself at the lid, hoping that maybe with enough force she could lift it... "AGH!" She roared in pain as she collided with the lid and went crumpling down to the floor. Her sides heaved, but she got herself up again.

"Stop, lass!" Angus then interrupted firmly. "You're only going to get yourself more hurt, and then where will we be?" He persuaded.

"We have to get out!" She growled in return, settling into another crouch to jump.

"Aye, I agree with that, but this isn't going to help!" Angus insisted, placing a calming talon on her shoulder.

Her head whipped towards him at the touch, but a wave of pain from her arm distracted her from the many retorts that bubbled into mind. "This lid... It's going to have to come off sometime. And when it does, we flee!"

Angus continued to look at her pleadingly. "Azara, your arm—"

Then suddenly, the stone above them rustled, and both of them froze.

And watched as the stone lid opened above them.

10

Never Trust Business Suits

Isis slowly opened her eyes, the first thing she saw being an icy blue dragon.

"...Mppmmmhhhhh..." She groaned, trying to get her mouth to formulate words, but everything just felt so blurry. "Whhhhrrrrr.... Whhheeerrreeeee..."

The icy blue dragon quickly looked down at her, revealing her magnificent dual-colored eyes. "Please," she whispered in a meek voice.

"Please, you have to be very, very quiet right now," she begged.

Isis groggily stared up at her, and saw the fear swirling in the eyes that looked beseechingly down at her, and she understood, and kept quiet. The ice colored dragon then looked in the direction she had originally been looking. Isis followed her gaze.

To where a pair of metal doors were slowly sliding open. Isis watched intently as human figures started filing into the room behind the glass.

They made a loose line in front of the cage, staring in at them, all with a stance of power. They all wore suits like the people that had captured them, but they were more...

Political looking.

Business people. Politicians.

Never trust business suits... Her thoughts echoed.

There were four of them, two men and two women. Isis studied them with a trained eye— their hairstyles, their choice in suit, their facial expression, their posture, the very way they stood. She had learned as a leader of the Egyptians to analyze people like this, determine who they were and what they wanted, and what their intentions were. For there was one thing that a business suit signified: These people were never quite who they said they were.

"The Queen of England would never approve of this," the first one said, a sturdy looking woman of moderate height and brown hair. She wore a simple black suit with a jacket and skirt, her hair simple and down. Her accent was British.

"Well that's why Britain has a Prime Minister then, isn't it?" A tall, gaunt man pointed out. He had buzz-cut gray hair and a very slim figure, and wore a matching slim grey suit and blue tie. He looked vaguely Russian.

Perhaps he is, Isis thought. *Leaders... They look like leaders...*

"Well I think it's brilliant. It's exactly the solution we need." A stocky man with Asian features joined in. He had a very square face and black hair to match his black suit and red tie.

"But how exactly will this work? There's billions of them out there— it would be like trying to catch every mouse in the world and putting them all in cages." A woman with olive skin and wavy black hair asked. She wore an elegant white suit and had a bland accent— definitely American.

"We don't need to catch all of them— just enough. Just the important ones," the Keeper assured.

The brown-haired lady frowned. "Wouldn't that cause the reverse effect of what we're trying to achieve with this?" She questioned.

"My boss will explain everything to you. We just wanted to show you the prototype—"

"Speaking of your boss," the tall slim man interrupted, "When do we get to meet the ever so secretive designer of this program?" He asked carefully.

The Keeper remained calm and cool. "My boss is currently occupied. I'm sure that the next time we meet they will have time to speak with you and answer all of your questions."

The Chinese man didn't look all too thrilled. "Are you saying that you've gathered all the major world powers in one room in your place, and your boss can't make time to meet with us?" In fact, he sounded quite furious.

The Keeper did not seem thrown. "My boss is a very busy person. I assure you that they are not here for a very good reason," he explained, then turned to face the cage again. "The Habitat has the capacity to comfortably hold five thousand pocket dragons. They will be well cared for with a healthy diet, sanitary conditions and medical care with mechanical efficiency."

Five thousand dragons.... Isis groggily thought. *Why do they need a cage to hold five thousand dragons...?* She wondered.

The American woman narrowed her eyes as she peered into the glass. "You said there would be a hundred dragons for demonstration. I hardly see ten."

The Keeper again had an answer. "I assure you ma'am that there are a hundred dragons. We have shelters and hiding places built in to The Habitat to make them feel safe and secure, just like in their natural habitat. It is likely that many of them are hiding right now, which is a perfectly natural behavior. Dragons are like mice: they like places to hide."

The woman didn't look completely assured, but both men were nodding approvingly.

The Keeper then continued. "So if you would all follow me, we can continue our tour," he said, and then proceeded to lead the world leaders out through a second set of metal doors that Isis hadn't noticed before.

As soon as the humans filed through the door and it clinked shut, closing them off from view, the habitat exploded with dragons.

Panicked, chaotic dragons, throwing themselves against the glass, digging at the grass and dirt, all trying to escape. All desperate to find some way out of wherever they were now, none of them succeeding.

The only one who didn't join the frenzy was the icy dragon above her.

"What.... Happened...." She croaked, her voice finally starting to return to her. "Where... Are we?"

The dragoness looked down at her with her piecing, fearful eyes, then said: "It will take a while to explain," she started. "But this place... The humans call it The Habitat..." She took a breath. "But... I'm calling it The Glass Cage.

11

How to Train your Human

Light shined down upon them as the lid was removed from the stone box.

"We present to you, William Bronze, your dragons," an elderly male voice boomed.

Angus squinted, trying to make out the figures in the light above him. Even Azara had halted in the midst of her escape attempts.

Above them was the face of a boy, peering down at them.

A young boy, around the age of twelve.

The boy had a long, angular face for his age, and caramel brown hair. His bright green eyes stared curiously down at them, just as Angus stared curiously up at the boy.

"Hello there," the boy said warmly, bracing a hand on the rim of the box.

He prayed that Azara wouldn't bolt.

Yet of course, in her typical fashion as Angus had come to know in their short time together, she did exactly that.

She blasted off into the air in a blur of blue scales. Angus tried to lunge and pin down her tail, but he was too slow. Above him, the boy flashed out a hand, and caught Azara before she could get any further, holding her in a firm but gentle fist. The human child seemed more intrigued that intent on hurting them.

Please be quiet please be quiet don't make these people mad at us I don't want to die here please be quiet—

"Let me GO!" Azara roared.

Angus decided he would stop hoping for Azara to not do something, as it only seemed to jinx them.

The boy cocked his head. "I can't do that. You are my dragons," he said, sounding truly and innocently miffed at the idea.

The child then looked back down into the box, down at Angus. Angus held his breath as the boy slowly reached down a hand. He used all of his will not to run and scamper and fly—it would do him little good, and he let the boy's fingers close around him and lift him up.

"William Bronze," The elderly voice commanded, "These dragons are more than just your pets: they are your companions through life and after then. Even so, they are your responsibility. You must care for them as if they were your own family, your own kin, your own children. You must never neglect in your care of them," the man boomed. "Do you promise to uphold to these promises so long as you shall live?" Angus twisted his neck to see the owner of the voice— an old man, yet not the one who had bought them. This one's beard was long, and by the way of his dress, he almost looked like a wizard in white, complete with a robe and a hat— though the latter looked more like a fancy sleeping cap.

William nodded. "Yes sir, I promise," he confirmed, and he sounded sincere.

"Also keep in mind that these dragons can offer you great wisdom. I have been informed that they are young— almost your age in our years but they are adults in theirs. If your dragons choose to grace you with their voice, then you should do well to listen."

Again, William nodded. "Yes sir."

The old man smiled, the edges of his eyes crinkling. He raised his arms above his head. "Then it is time to celebrate!" He announced, and cheerful music promptly started. He then looked down at the boy again. "Have fun, and get to know your dragons," he encouraged.

The boy lifted Angus and Azara closer to his face to look at them. He turned to Azara first. "Do you have a name?" He asked curiously.

Angus wasn't sure how Azara hadn't passed out yet from the pain of having her arm squished. Yet it was clearly enough to have her distracted— all she could formulate in response was a growl.

"Are you alright?" The boy now asked, suddenly looking concerned.

The slow, deadly glare that Azara gave him was priceless.

His hand slowly unfurled, and Azara must have been in so much pain that she couldn't even think to escape then, for she made no move to do so. The boy carefully inspected her, his eyes going right for her arm.

"You're injured..." He realized aloud. The boy set Angus down on his shoulder to free his hand, and Angus was too concerned for Azara to make an escape attempt of his own. He perched on the boy's shoulder and peered down at the blue dragoness. William gently examined the arm with his now free hand. Azara winced. "It's broken," the boy diagnosed.

Apparently the elder had heard him. "Broken? This is an outrage! We must— " the wizard-man fumed.

But Will cut him off. "It's alright sir— I can mend it! I know how to heal her," he insisted. Before the elder could protest, the boy had turned and started sprinting towards the stone house.

Angus had to dig his claws into the thick russet shirt of the boy to hang on. As the boy ran, Angus caught quick glances of the village around them. The town square had indeed been set up for a ceremony— and from the looks of it, every person in the village had come. Many people were dancing or eating or playing. Many people, Angus noticed, also sported dragons riding upon their shoulders or riding in chest pockets or hovering nearby. Yet there was a certain... Look to them that was just... Off. It took a moment for Angus to recognize what it was.

They looked exactly like the dragons from the store.

Despite being out of a cage, despite being so close to freedom should they wish it, they all looked so... hopeless. They looked trapped, as if the real cage wasn't one of glass or steel, but from within.

Angus didn't get to see any more, as soon as they were at the door of the house. William swung the door open and sprinted inside. Angus got a good look of the simple entry room, which contained a plain white sofa, a firepit in a cobblestone hearth, and a low table between the two. To the left there was a basic kitchen. In front of him, Angus saw a wooden staircase on one side of the wall paralleling the door, then another door on the other end of the wall.

Apparently, the boy was heading for that very door. It was painted sky blue with a bronze doorknob. William twisted the doorknob and rushed inside.

This, Angus presumed, was the boy's room.

Two large windows let light shine into the room, illuminating it. There was a child-sized bed with pillows and blankets, a carpet, a desk, and....

A cage.

It was like a large birdcage— large enough for a parrot if not two. The walls were glass and it went all the way up to the ceiling. Dead center, there was a fake yet highly detailed tree that spiraled up to the top. Angus noticed that there were several holes that led perhaps inside the tree.

It took up at least a third of the boy's little room.

The boy kneeled beside the table that the cage stood upon. Not bothering to remove

Angus from his shoulder, the boy gently laid Azara out on the wooden table. He then proceeded to quickly collect assorted supplies from compartments that he kept nearby.

Angus watched intently as Will spread out these supplies for him to use, all for fixing and casting a broken bone. Will looked about to begin, but Azara snarled.

The boy flinched, drawing back his hand. *Please Azara... This boy can help you then we can escape! You just need to let him help you!* He mentally urged, though he knew she couldn't hear him. The odds of that were... Extremely low.

Yet, to his relief, she didn't struggle or growl when the boy went to start again. She endured it all, and not a while later she had her arm wrapped up in a makeshift miniature cast and sling with a strap that went between her wings so that she could still fly.

When he had finished, William then opened the hatch into the glass cage. Azara started backing up, but Will scooped her up before she could make a hasty escape. The boy reached up with his free hand and plucked Angus off from his shoulder. He then set them both down inside the cage, and quickly closed the hatch before Azara could turn and lunge for it.

Yet this time, Azara looked more despaired than angry. More like she was just tired of being put in a cage than angry at it...

She was starting to look like those dragons who he had seen at the store, at the ceremony. It was frustrating how reckless she was.... *But this... This is worse... We can't give up hope...*

Azara shot him a glare. It was a couple seconds before she finally said: "So you wanted me not to run. So I didn't. Now what? We're in a cage again," she growled.

Angus turned and scanned the cage, curious about those potential entrances that he had spotted earlier. "We can't do anything until your arm is healed," he said, then promptly spread his wings and jumped into the air.

"And then what?" Azara asked, beating her wings to follow him. "We just politely ask to be let free? I know about this sort of culture. This boy has been raised to think of dragons as pets— he's not going to let us go unless our lives depended on it."

Angus glided to a landing into one of the entrances. Azara was right behind him. "He seems fairly sincere in his desire to take care of us," Angus pointed out as he explored down the little passageway into the tree trunk. The area then opened up to a large living space that was very intricately decorated. There were two dragon-sized nests made of cotton and cloth, there were little tables and little wooden boxes that contained everything ranging from what looked like food to toys. There were even little windows in the tree with perfect nooks to curl up and fall asleep in. Everything looked carefully, lovingly handcrafted. "I think he might even help us beyond just letting us go if need be," he added.

"And how do you know that?" Azara questioned, still glaring at him. "You've literally just met him!"

Angus nodded at the room, and finally Azara turned her head to look at it. She glanced over the room with reluctant understanding. "He put this much work into preparing for us. I think he would help us, said he.

Azara bit her lip. "It would appear so." She turned to him again. "But how? How can we get him to trust us enough that when we say we need to go gallivanting off to the Dragon Queen, he'll help us?"

Angus grinned. "We do what all clever felines do to their humans," he said.

"We train him."

12

Mission to Willough

"Can you explain to me, why, Mr. S, the dragons were late?" The Keeper growled in a low voice. The gruff man had a name like any other human, but like Mr. S, he never actually told anyone what that was. Mr. S was a tall, slim, young man in his mid twenties with Asian features.

Unlike The Keeper, however, Mr. S rarely showed any emotion at all. He remained completely calm as he answered. "It took a while to collect them all. Some of the dragons you needed wouldn't fall for traps: they had to be hand-caught. Others were from rather far away. I don't know if you've ever been dragon snatching, but it takes a while to import a hundred dragons from all over Europe and farther. We even had one from New York," he said. They were in a corridor right outside The Habitat— their visitors had recently left. Despite being inside, Mr. S kept his shades on— it was best not be recognized by anyone, even his co-workers. It was safer that way.

"Not even a hundred," The Keeper corrected. "We have all the dragons in The Habitat now and there were only ninety-nine. We reminded the doctor that he couldn't treat any of that batch when we saw there weren't as many as there should be, but in the end there were only ninety-nine."

Mr. S didn't even furrow his brows in confusion. "That is impossible. We brought in one hundred and one: we brought in a surplus," he argued.

The Keeper tensed. "Don't lie to me. There were ninety-nine drag— "

A set of beeps went off from his wrist, cutting off the fuming Keeper. Mr. S raised his wrist up to inspect the black watch he wore on it. There was a screen fitted atop it, showing the time digitally. He tapped the screen with his other hand, and the time blurred away. The watches were The Lab's main way of long communication, and they used a secure channel that was undetectable. Words in light blue appeared on the dark blue screen background. Mr. S read the message then tapped his watch again to erase it. He lifted his head to the Keeper again. "The dragons have been sold before they were treated. I must retrieve them," he said curtly, then turned to leave and complete his assignment.

"Bring Clara with you," the Keeper called from behind him.

Mr. S paused. "Sir, Clara is half the reason we were late bringing the dragons in. Need I mention how many times she accidentally let them loose when feeding them?" He objected. "She wasted a week if not more of having to go and catch them again. She has no control."

"Bring her, S," The Keeper ordered. "She may be reckless, but she is still good at snatching. She caught a dozen dragons with her bare hands in one week. You've caught one with your hands, ever."

"I'm better with the traps, sir. It was my idea after all to set up traps with recordings as lures. As well as to offer 'free pest traps' to farmers. I've caught seventy-two dragons that way."

He had a feeling that the Keeper was turning red behind him. "I don't care how many dragons you caught with your contraptions! Those aren't going to work with capturing dragons that are already in a cage. Bring Clara."

"Yes sir," Mr. S. forced through his teeth, and began quickly walking down the corridor. "Now if you will excuse me, I have some dragons to retrieve from Willough."

13

Frostfire

Frida shifted her wings, clinging to the trunk of the tree with her little talons. She dug her claws into the hard, dry bark, and resisted the urge to peer around, to glance at the other dragons similarly clinging to the treetops around the vent in the roof. She tried not to act as if the entire glass cage was filled with tension, pretending to find a knot in the tree bark very interesting. She didn't know if the plan would work— it wasn't the first, yet they all hoped it would be the last.

She shuffled her wings again to signal that she was ready. Several other dragons around the ring of trees did the same. Only about two-dozen of them were perching as she was now, ready to carry out the plan— it had been decided earlier that the attempt would be less conspicuous with fewer dragons loitering around near the tunnel. She found herself kneading the bark with one claw as she thought of how, of all dragons, she should not be on the escape mission. *I'm by far the most likely to get caught again... Or worse... Get everyone else caught again...* She thought. Yet that golden dragon, Isis, had insisted that she go. The beautiful dragon hadn't given her any time since then to refuse or back out and let someone else more worthy take her place.

Isis had even remained on the ground, choosing to stay behind, so that she might look after the other remaining dragons. It was primarily the elders, who knew that the younger, swifter dragons would have the best chance, that made up the majority of the population staying behind.

Frida took a calming breath. The dragons had no precise knowledge of when the tunnel would open, yet it was always in the morning, so for now all they could do was wait.

At least, they thought it was in the morning. The lights in the lab were never turned off, leaving them in an eternal, timeless day. Some dragons tried to keep the time— the many small claw-marks in the trees of countless hours gone by marked that they had been there for at least a fortnight. Yet they could never tell for sure.

It certainly didn't feel like two weeks. It felt like a month. A season. A year. Nothing but the same trees, the same leaves, the same disgusting food. If Isis hadn't been there to guide them, collect them, she knew that many more dragons would have given in to despair by now. Herself likely included.

The sound of an engine whirring into life sounded above them, along with the sound of blasting and whistling winds. The snouts of all the dragons snapped up at the familiar sound that always preceded the opening of the tunnel.

Not a moment later, the vent snapped open, radiating neon blue light.

And in that very same moment, Frida and the other dragons launched themselves from the trees. Frida beat her wings towards the shrieking winds, the blare blasting down upon them. The force of the wind blasted against her, blowing her down, away from the entrance.

The force was too strong for her... *I'm not going to make it...* She realized. Around her, other dragons were also struggling, only a few managing to get within a few inches of the entrance. She must have been less than a foot away, but her wings had to beat furiously to keep her not only aloft but moving up.... And her energy was quickly draining.

Then in a flash of neon and scales, there were dragons raining upon them. Frida instantly let herself drop— just in time to miss a turquoise and white dragon from colliding into her.

The awful sound of scales cracking and bones crunching told her that others weren't so lucky. As she fell, she saw dragons falling together with terribly disfigured limbs from crashing into each other. One dragon was missing his horns entirely, whereas she saw another dragon with a horn embedded into his flank.

Frida hit the firm ground so hard that all the breath was knocked from her lungs. The world spun for a moment as her own struggling breath echoed in her ears. The blurry figure of a golden dragon appeared above her, concernedly but calmly scanning over her. "Are you alright?" She asked.

Her vision slowly stopped spinning enough for her to nod her head. "I'll be fine," she choked.

Isis nodded, then offered a talon to help her up. Frida accepted it and heaved herself back to her talons. "Can you go around and see which dragons are most in need of healing attention?" The golden dragon asked.

Frida gave her a nod. "Yes." The golden dragon gave her a thankful smile then turned to assist the other dragons.

Frida turned to do as she was instructed, going around and searching for injured dragons scattered around the area. *Isis is so brilliant...* She thought as she went around, inquiring as to various dragon's state then continuing on after hearing they were fine. *She always knows just what to do... And she's always brave... Never afraid...* She got the sinking feeling in her stomach as she recalled that she was just he opposite. *I never know what to do. I always want to hide... I always shy away from opportunity while Isis... She leaps for it and holds on with all of her talons.*

She came across a dragon lying on her side, moaning. She realized that it was the turquoise and white dragon whom she had narrowly avoided crashing into just minutes ago. Her frame was thin and her horns were long. *She's old.* Frida realized. Her bones could have been damaged from the fall alone. Horns were a telltale sign of a dragon's age, most of the time. Like a human's hair, horns never stopped growing. It was slow, very slow, but a dragon in their late hundreds could have horns one, sometimes two inches long. She thought with a flinch of the dragon whose horns had been broken off. They would regrow, so really the only major injury he had suffered would be one to his pride, but it still couldn't have been pleasant considering some dragon's horns also contained veins, like a cat's claws.

"Are you alright?" She asked politely to the elderly turquoise dragoness on the ground.

"My... Wing..." The elder dragon groaned. Frida then noticed that the dragon's frail white wing was crushed awkwardly beneath her.

"Can you walk? There are dragons here who can heal. If you can walk I can bring you to them," she explained softly. Dragons were always coming in injured from the wind tunnel, so Isis had set up a system where they would group the ones who could wait, then see to the more critical injuries first. Frida guessed that there would be more of the latter this time, considering the multiple collisions due to the escape attempt.

She waited a moment, and the elderly dragoness gave a slow nod. Frida helped her to her talons and to hobble over to the forming group of dragons with injuries waiting to be healed.

She helped the elder get settled comfortably onto the grass, and was about to turn when she noticed that the dragoness looked as if she was... Wilting again. "Are you sure you are alright?" She asked.

The dragoness was sprawling herself out, stretching out her wings as if... As if trying to cool off. "It's.... So warm... In here...." She panted.

Frida raised her eye ridges. To her, accustomed to the frozen lands of Siberia, it did feel rather warm, though other dragons had informed her it was neutral. "Where are you from?" She asked.

"Ant.... Antarctica..." The elder panted, now trying to shade herself with her good wing as if it would do her any good.

She's built for the coldest of temperatures. To her, this place must be like a desert, she realized. From the pained state of the elder, she realized that this might as well be an alien planet for the elder. *She can't survive here... She needs cold....* "Do you have a cold magic that you could use to cool yourself?"

"I have.... Cold magic... But it won't work... In this heat..." The elder replied, sounding weaker by the second. Too long, and she might pass out... And never wake up.

She felt her own cold stir within her. She felt sparks churning in her core, then flowing through her mouth. A gentle flow of icy blue flame blew from her jaws, washing over the elder like a mist. She kept the steady flow going, her core trained from maintaining huge fires back in Siberia to be able to hold a steady firebreath for almost as long as she could go without oxygen— a couple hours, sometimes more.

A few dragons around her watched in wonder. A couple noticed with horror until they realized something quite peculiar about the flame.

It emitted no heat. In fact, it emanated cold. It was a frostfire— a cold flame.

She let the cold flames wash over the elder for a good few minutes, then withdrew her fire, and instead widened the firefall from her jaws, letting the fire spread over a decent portion of the ground, leaving it coated in frost and ice. She then concentrated it once again, until she left a cold fire burning near the elder, emanating cold.

By the time she finally snapped her snout shut, she realized that almost every dragon nearby had paused, and turned, to look at her.

At her cold fire, cooling off the elder from the south. The turquoise dragon slowly lifted her head, opened her eyes, and surveyed the miniature winterland around her. Wonder, awe, such.... Simple happiness showed through the elder's eyes when she finally turned her elegant face to look at Frida again. "Thank you," the turquoise dragon said, her voice almost wobbling.

All around her, dragons of frost and ice origin stumbled towards the cold flame. Slowly, surrounding her, drawn towards her cold fire. Frida looked around at every face around her, timid at the feeling of them all looking towards her. She had never.... Never been thanked quite like that before. Kostya and the others from her village had thanked her, but the elder dragoness... She sounded as if Frida had been the first light she had seen in a long, dark tunnel. She wasn't sure what to do, if she should say anything, if she should turn and hide...

She felt a gust of air as the golden dragon landed beside her, her bright sun-colored scales particularly beautiful against the crisp icy blues and silvers and whites. Isis looked around in wonder at the scene before her stunning green eyes finally landed on Frida. "Did you know you could do this?" She asked gently.

Frida hesitated a second, but then gave a nod. "Yes... I never used it much though... I didn't think it would ever be useful..." She murmured.

Isis smiled. "You've done a wonderful thing, Frida. Now, at least, more dragons have a better chance of surviving, and that's all because of you."

Frida wanted to protest— *I haven't done anything, really. I just have a peculiar and usually useless extra form of fire that just happened to be useful...* But Isis continued before she could say anything.

"I think..." Isis slowly scanned around at the dragons around them. "I think we'll take a break from the escape attempts. Let these dragons heal, look after the new ones. Study the humans more and figure out their bigger plans— so that when we finally do escape, we can make a difference," she said decidedly. The regal dragoness then turned her head back to Frida, her expression... Curious, thoughtful. As if Frida might actually be useful in some way.... Something else she was not used to seeing. "Frida," the golden dragon then said, "I want you to be in charge of the frost dragons. You can keep them cold and help them survive while we're trapped here. You are one of them— they will listen to you more than they will me. Even if we're in a cage right now, we cannot give way to disorder and become the animals they think we are. We need to stand united, and you can help with that. I've already appointed several other leaders— forest dragons, water dragons, and I think you would be perfect for the frost dragons." She explained.

Frida wanted to shrink. "I-I don't know how—"

"You'll do fine," Isis cut her off in assurance. The golden dragon spread her wings, ready to return to healing the other wounded dragons. She jumped into the air, but then she paused, hovering. "Frida," she added.

"Yes?" Frida asked, hoping the trembling in her voice wasn't all that audible.

Isis smiled, then said before swooping away:

"Your eyes, they are very beautiful."

14
An Unexpected Escape

Azara slowly awoke, feeling a beam of sunlight drifting over her snout and face and warming them. She stretched out her good legs, enjoying the comfort of the soft fluffy nest beneath her. *No,* she suddenly reprimanded herself. *I will not enjoy a pet's luxuries.* Her eyes snapped open as she jolted completely awake and to her talons. In a nearby nest, Angus appeared to also be waking.

"It's not as good as sheep.... But at least it doesn't travel..." The green dragon said, stretching out like a cat.

Azara shook her head in dismay, then glanced down at her arm. The cast could come off soon, her bone already feeling mostly healed. Her memory flashed to the sound of the voice of that one woman... Back in the room with the man in a white coat. *"Their bones have got to be like, this tiny! It can't take that long to heal."* The voice had said. Indeed, their light, hollow yet strong bones were tiny, but it was not because of that that they healed swiftly— it was because of the magic in their blood that mended injuries more efficiently.

She flexed her wings, starting towards one of the many passageways that led out of the fake tree that was their new temporary home. For two weeks now they had been trying to work with Will, wordlessly showing him that he could trust them and how smart they were.... Even when escape was just a carelessly open window away.

But Angus insisted that they wait until her arm was healed. She hated to agree, but... Embarking on a quest would be hard enough in peak physical condition. So she let herself be handled and petted and locked in a cage at night... The boy wasn't cruel or mean to them, but sometimes.... She wanted to give one of his fingers a nip on the off chance it might make him smarter. William was kind... Though his understanding of dragons was... Flawed.

The tunnel gave way to the open area outside, yet still within the confines of the cage. False grass covered the ground inside the cage, and a bowl with water was inset into the earthen ground to create the effect of a pool. The locked hatch remained the only way out. Azara landed by the pool of water and dipped her head down to take a drink. As she lapped at the cool water, she got the odd.... sense...

That she was being.... watched. She took one last gulp, then raised her head.

There, sitting right outside the cage, was an umber brown dragon.

Azara eyed him as he raised a talon to the glass, then... Tapped on it. Then again. He paused briefly, then resumed his tapping. One... Two... Three....

"Who is that?" Angus asked from behind her, startling her as he landed.

Azara was too intrigued by the number dragon to jump. "I don't know..." She replied in a half-transfixed fashion, curious about the tapping. She cocked her head and slowly wandered towards the dragon on the other side of the glass. He was male, she could see, with pale yellow horns and wings.

"What is he saying?" Angus asked curiously, his voice still drowsy from having just woken up.

"I'm.... Not sure," she replied. She sat down on the cool grass and studied his tapping. *It's clearly a pattern.... A code....* She thought. *It's just a matter of which one...*

Tap tap, he paused, *tap tap tap*. He took a longer pause, then *tap tap,* shorter pause, *tap tap tap tap.*

She racked her memory of books from the many museum gift shops that she had read by night.

Tap tap, tap tap tap, a long pause, *tap tap, tap tap tap*. The brown dragon repeated.

He's trying to say something.... She listened to the tapping, listened to the umber dragon... He looked so desperate for her to understand...

"He doesn't go over five," Angus commented from behind her. She had almost forgotten he was there.

Azara furrowed her brows, then suddenly it came to her. "It's a tap code!" She realized, her eyes wide with the thrill of the discovery.

Angus slid over to sit beside her. "Yeeeeeees that's apparent lass," he said sarcastically.

Azara shook her head. "No— it's literally called a Tap Code. It's a five-by-five code often used by prisoners to communicate in secret," she rapidly explained.

Angus raised his brows. "Now how did you know that?" He asked.

She shook her head in dismissal. "I.... Read books. Not important. What is important is that I think I can understand him." She inched forward so that she was within arm's reach of the glass.

Azara nodded, encouraging the umber dragon to try again. He lifted his talon, and tapped.... Once, twice, pause, once, twice, thrice.

"H!" Azara announced, calculating the code in her head.

The umber dragon rapidly nodded, then continued. Tap, tap, pause, tap, tap, tap, tap.

"I!" Azara figured out. "Hi! He said hi." She said to Angus excitedly. She turned back to the umber dragon. "Hello," she said in return.

From there, the dragon's taps quickened, as if worried about running out of time. Azara listened intently and calculated each letter. *.... Y .... O .... U .... F .... R .... O .... M .... L .... A .... B...* The dragon then cocked his head in question.

"You from lab?" Azara repeated aloud, and the umber dragon nodded. *I guess technically that place... Whatever it was... It could be described as a Lab.* She glanced at Angus again before replying to the brown dragon: "Yes, we were there before we were... Bought and taken here." He looked ready to tap another question, but she had one of her own. "Why can't you speak?" She asked.

An air of sadness surrounded the brown dragon, but he swiftly tapped: *.... L .... A .... B .... T ... O ... O ....* Yet by the time he had tapped once more, the sound of footsteps on creaky wood startled the umber dragon, and he began to rapidly retreat.

"No! Wait! What were you saying!" Azara called desperately. But the umber dragon only frantically shook his head, and leapt off the table. He was just disappearing out the open window when the blue door slid open and a human figure stepped in.

William strolled in, and, seeing them sitting by the edge of the cage, kneeled by them. "Hello," he greeted, smiling. "Good afternoon. Dragons really do love their sleep, don't they?" He playfully joked.

Azara glanced up at the boy, then her memory hit her and she quickly turned to Angus. "Are you ready?" She asked in a rushed whisper. In her fascination with the umber dragon, she had completely forgotten about their plan for today.

The green dragon nodded. "Your arm is almost healed— now is the best time," he said decidedly.

"Alright," She agreed. The two of them made their way towards the area below the hatch, then waited.

"Want to come out?" He asked, already reaching to unlatch the hatch. They had trained him to let them out whenever they went there, getting him to trust that they wouldn't fly away.

He would be completely unsuspecting when they actually did.

At least, Azara was still heart set on that plan. Angus remained determined to get the boy to do more than just let them out— maybe take them all the way to London. A multi-day flight sounded fine to her, but Angus seemed more used to catching a ride.

The hatch clicked and the boy lifted it open. The dragons spread their wings and lifted up through the open hatch, then landed on the wooden table that the cage was set on. "Want your breakfast?" Will asked, producing a wrapped-up napkin from his pocket. He gave a mischievous grin. "I sneaked you some of mine. Technically breakfast was about three hours ago, so it might be a little cold, but I think it's better than what my grandfather tells me to feed you," he added with an apologetic grimace, referring to the table-scrap-mystery-meat that he usually fed them. He unwrapped the napkin to reveal some chunks of boiled potato and poached egg and cheese. Will picked up a piece of potato between two fingers and offered it to her.

The potato looked delicious, and she could see the butter glinting off of it, but now was not the time to eat. She raised a talon and set it down on his finger, her talon barely larger than his fingernail. She gently pushed his hand down, diverting the attention from the food to between them— William looked thoroughly shocked by the action that he let her control.

She took a breath, getting a sense that the boy was holding his, then said: "Hello, Will."

Azara was jolted back as William practically rocketed backwards with a surprised "AHHH!" His back banged against his bed with an audible thwack, and a moment later several precariously placed books slid from a shelf above his bed and showered down upon him, conjuring another cry of surprise.

Azara heard a faint chuckle from behind her, and whipped her head around and glared at Angus. The green dragon immediately sealed his snout with an innocent look. *Oi vey*, she mentally muttered, and strolled over to the edge of the table. Angus followed her, perching on the edge and peering down.

Despite the pile of books scattered around him, William was in the exact same position he was in when he banged against the side of the bed. And he was staring right at them.

"Okay," Azara began promptly. "First things first. We're not your pets. Dragons aren't pets. Got that? Second, we need your help."

Angus gave her a sidelong glare. "Azara!" He whispered. "Weren't we going to, you know, take it slow?"

Azara glared right back at him. "That dragon was trying to tell us something about the lab! Clearly this problem is more widespread than we thought— we need to find out more, and find out how to stop it! And now! There's no time to waste!"

Both dragons turned their heads to face a trembling Will, who after a long moment, finally stuttered:

"Y-You can talk!"

And not a moment later, a ferocious banging sounded from the front door.

They all turned their heads, staring at the sky-blue door fearfully, listening to the events in the next room. They heard the creaking of the stairs as someone descended them, then footsteps as they crossed the main room.

"Hello?" An elderly voice asked as the screeching of hinges told them that the door was being opened. Azara recognized it as William's grandfather's voice.

"Good day sir," A male, strangely familiar voice said. "We have heard that this household is in possession of dragons. We are officials from the DPA, the Dragon Protection Agency. We make routine checks to ensure the sanitary and healthy conditions of dragons under human care. Would you show us the habitat of your dragons and allow us to make an inspection?"

There was a pause, and then: "Would you show me your badge?" The elderly man asked. There was another pause, then suddenly followed by the sound of a *slam!* "RUN WILLS!" The old man suddenly bellowed. Not half a second later there was an awful *crack*, and the sound of something falling to the floor.

Azara assumed it was the grandfather. She instantly turned back to Will. "Will! Hurry! We have to go!" She urged.

Will bolted to his feet. "But where?" He asked frantically. Footsteps sounded outside, heading towards the blue door.

"Out the window, obviously!" Azara replied. She leapt from the edge of the table and dived into his chest-pocket, Angus close behind.

"But— "

"NOW WILL!"

Azara scrambled to clutch the rim of the pocket and poke her head above so that she could see as Will shoved the window open further and began to climb through it.

A loud wooden *bang* sounded from behind him, and Azara knew it must be whoever it had been at the door. "Stop, boy!" A female voice demanded.

Azara recognized that voice. *Oh no,* she realized. *"Their bones have got to be this tiny!"* The memory of the voice echoed in her head. "The Lab has found us!" Azara yelled.

Yet her voice was washed out as she and Angus fell deeper into the pocket as William, without hesitating, launched himself out the window.

"Gah!" Azara complained as she was thrown about as William landed on the ground.

"Sorry!" Will apologized under his breath. Azara climbed to regain her previous vantage point as Will scrambled to his feet. 'What now?" He asked.

Around them, there was nothing but the small house behind them and the forest in front of them. The end of the blue truck poked out from behind the corner of the house. There was no one else from the village in sight.

Angus poked his head up, joining her. "Get in the truck!" Angus ordered. When the boy hesitated, he added, "you were told to listen to us, so listen to us now!"

The boy bolted for the truck, and Azara and Angus had to dig their talons into the cloth of the pocket to hand on and not get thrown out. "Wait, won't you need the car keys?!" Azara pointed out.

"My grandfather always leaves them in the car," Will panted. He swung around the side of the vehicle and threw open the door. In those brief couple seconds, they got a glance at the two people pursuing them.

Two humans, one male one female, of almost equal height and stature. One was a skinny male with Asian features and wore shades and a dark suit. The other was a lean female with unkempt black hair, black suit with an open jacket revealing a black tank top beneath, and her shades hung loosely on her nose. The woman pointed a thin finger at them. "Stop right there kid!" She yelled.

William stared at them for a moment longer before jumping into the car and slamming the door closed. He then desperately groped around for the key. "Where is it where is it where is it!" He muttered.

She and Angus climbed out of his pocket and swiftly flew to various parts of the car looking for the keys, poking into little compartments in the dashboard and below the seats and between them. "So I thought that old wizard guy said to listen to us when we talk. Why were you surprised when we did?" Azara asked absentmindedly as she rapidly dug through an overhead compartment.

William threw up his hands in frustration from the search. "They just say that as a tradition. The dragons of Willough haven't spoken in years," he answered. Azara might have thought more on the subject, but was interrupted by:

"I found them!" Angus suddenly called, and came flapping in from a compartment in the dashboard, carrying the keys.

Azara glided down from where she had been searching and hovered above the passenger seat, Angus following suit soon after depositing the keys in the boy's hand.

William jammed the keys into the slot by the wheel, furiously trying the many different keys. Finally one of them clicked, and he turned it to lock it.

"Well, drive!" Angus urged.

William placed his hands on the wheel, but froze. "I don't know how! I'm only twelve! I've never driven a car before!"

Azara slapped her forehead with a talon. "There's a foot pedal! Press it and it makes you go forward!" She instructed. She had spent enough time sneaking into cars to catch rides that she knew that much about human vehicles.

Suddenly, there was a knock on the glass. "AHHHHHHHHHHH!" They all screamed as they saw it was the man in the dark suit.

"Get out of the car and we won't hurt you," he said, his voice muffled through the glass.

Still staring at the man through the glass, Will slammed his foot onto the pedal.

The car lurched, causing them all to jerk forward, but the car remained stationary. Azara rolled her eyes. "The other one!" She yelled.

The man outside looked ready to lunge as William switched his foot to the other pedal, and slammed that one down.

The car went wildly zooming forward, straight towards the forest. Angus and Azara slammed into the passenger seat and crumbled down, landing on the base of the seat. "What now!?" Will asked as they sped towards the trees.

Azara scrambled to her talons and climbed onto the arm of the seat. "Drive away!" She said.

"Well obviously, but how?!" William asked desperately, his frantic gaze darting from between the dragons and the looming trees.

Azara poked her head around the corner of the seat, and saw the two agents climbing into their own sleek black vehicle. "I don't know, try to lose them in the woods!" She shouted back. With another glance behind them, she saw that the black car was already speeding towards them. "Quickly!"

"I don't know how to drive!" William repeated. Trees flashed past them as they broke the tree line into the forest, narrowly missing several by just a few inches.

SNAP!

The left side-mirror smashed and snapped off when it was rammed into a tree. "My grandfather won't like that!" William shouted.

BANG!

They all slowly turned to look at the hole in the back window, causing the window to fragment into a million tiny pieces and slowly crumble away.

"THAT IS A BULLET!" William yelled horrifiedly. "THAT IS A BLOODY BULLET!" He glanced terrifiedly down at them. "Would someone please explain to me why we're being chased by people in creepy black suits who are SHOOTING AT US?"

"It's a long story!" Azara replied. "One we'd be happy to tell as soon as— "

CRASH!

Tiny fragments of glass flew everywhere as the back window completely exploded.

They all turned to look through the now completely open window, straight at the alarming black car chasing them. The woman with the wild hair was hanging half out of her window with a handgun trained on them.

"What do we do?!" Will yelled in panic.

Azara racked her brains, trying to think of some way out of this impossible situation, when suddenly Angus roared: "NOT DRIVE INTO THAT TREE!"

William and Azara turned their heads back towards the front of the car just in time to see them speeding right towards a thick, wide tree.

They all screamed.

"AHHHHHHHHHHHHHHHHHHHHH HHHHHHH— "

CRUNCH!

They were all thrown forward as the car slammed into the tree, when suddenly everything exploded in whiteness.

Azara then heard Angus yell: "THE SHEEP HAVE COME! THEY ARE TAKING OVER THE WORLD! I KNEW THIS DAY WOULD CO— "

"HUSH! IT'S THE AIRBAGS!" Azara roared at wherever he may be in the maze of plastic whiteness.

"Oh." Angus sounded vaguely disappointed.

POP!

Azara saw that several airbags had been suddenly deflated in what appeared to be the back seat of the truck. She then heard William yell: "We're still being shot at! We need to get out of here!" Not a moment later, she felt his hand close around her, and she let him grasp her as he grabbed Angus with the other hand and kicked open the door.

Out in the open, there was nothing but massive trees and plants all around them.

And the black car, only a few hundred feet away and rapidly closing the distance.

She looked up at Will, and commanded: "RUN!"

15

No Method to the Madness

Clara hung half out of her window as Mr. S drove over the bumpy forest ground. She had her handgun pointed at the blue truck wildly driving ahead of them, and she made a shot every time the blue vehicle came into view. She ended up leaving a bunch of trees and plants with holes in them, but she had so far managed to at least blast the truck's back window through.

"Your shooting is erratic: Aim for the tires and they'll be stopped," Mr. S called to her from inside the car.

"Your driving is erratic!" She retorted. With her free hand she pinned a stray hair behind her ear before clamping both hands back down on her gun to steady her aim. "I assure you, there is a method to my madness."

Mr. S's attention remained focused on not ramming their fancy vehicle into a tree while still chasing down the lost dragons. "No, I do not believe there is," he replied. They had not anticipated that a twelve-year-old boy would be so adamant in keeping his dragons that he would take off through the woods in a car.

Screaming sounded from the truck ahead and was abruptly cut off as they drove right into a broad tree. The inside exploded into whiteness as the airbags inflated. "See?!" She pointed out. Clara made another shot at the exploded back of the car, deflating some of the airbags.

"That was random chance," Mr. S replied through gritted teeth.

Clara was about to make another shot at the back of the truck when the door flew open and the boy hopped out. He briefly turned to glance at them, and half a second later he was bolting through the woods.

"AFTER HIM!" Clara commanded at Mr. S.

"Now focus," Mr. S reprimanded. "Don't kill the boy— that will look bad. We just need to slow him down."

Clara proceeded to ignore him, firing randomly after the child as he sprinted over roots and plants and uneven terrain. Their car jerked up and down and left and right as it went over bumps and rocks and dodged to avoid trees. "WATCH YOUR DRIVING!" Clara shouted into the car. Yet then something ahead caught her eye.

A river.

It was small, no wider than two or three yards, but the depth was impossible to tell. "AFTER THEM! HURRY!! IF THEY CROSS THAT RIVER THEN WE'LL LOSE 'EM!" Clara yelled at Mr. S.

The boy was clearly running as fast as he could, leaping over rocks and branches. He too must have seen the river and what it meant if he crossed it.

Clara fired at him sporadically, narrowly missing him by inches in some places.

There were barely five-dozen yards left yet till the river. *We're going to miss them!!!* Clara realized. She slipped back inside to the car. "Give me the wheel!" She demanded.

Mr. S gave her a brief glance. "No. What are you doing? Get back to shooting. If you had slowed him down like I told you to we would have had him by now."

The car made a giant lurch as it ran over a large root. "Just give me the wheel!" She urged, and didn't wait for an answer. She lunged for the wheel, causing the car to careen around as Mr. S was slammed into the door.

"Let go!" Mr. S commanded urgently with his usual lack of expression.

"No you let go! Let me have the wheel! I can get them!" She argued. She felt a sharp jab to the ribs as he elbowed her, but she held tight, struggling for the wheel. Their fancy black car swerved left and right, narrowly missing trees and losing proximity to the boy. She finally turned her head from trying to pry Mr. S's hands from the wheel to see the boy just on the bank. "NOOOOOOOOOOOO!" She yelled, and yanked control of the vehicle and steered it straight towards the running boy.

The boy jumped.

He sailed over the river, and landed solidly on the other side. He didn't waste any time before he took off at a run again.

Clara saw a tiny blob of deep green and gold climbing up the boy's shoulder. She then realized it was a dragon... And it was waving its tiny black talons at her. *Waving them. At. Her.*

She was so distracted by her rage at the dragon that she hadn't been watching the ground, and only looked as Mr. S choked: "Clara—!"

And their car nosedived into the river.

"Get out! Get out!" Clara yelled, jumping for her side of the car where the window was already rolled down. Water was already gurgling through the open gap, and she desperately began to climb through. She heard the sound of glass shattering behind her as Mr. S broke his own window, followed by a surge of water.

She scrabbled out the window and jumped into the river. Icy cold water soaked her through as she plunged beneath the surface and her feet touched the sandy bottom. Clara pushed off, swimming back for the surface.

Her head broke the water, and she took a breath before glaring at the half-sunken car damming the little river.

She didn't bother to check if her partner had made it out, and swam to the opposite bank. She hauled herself out of the water, the cold wind suddenly biting and her suit feeling twenty pounds heavier from the water.

Mr. S was already standing on the bank, dripping wet, his mouth in a thin line. "Now look what you've done," he accused monotonously, pointing a finger at the sunken vehicle. Clara was still climbing out of the river.

"If you had just listened to me and—"

"Shut up!" She snapped, finally stumbling onto dry land. "In all of your logic, you've failed to notice that the kid is getting away!" She pointed out, aiming a finger towards where the boy's red shirt flashed in the distance, popping out between the greens and browns.

Mr. S didn't wait for her as he bolted into the woods, but Clara wasn't far behind. In a matter of seconds she was ahead of him and leaving him behind. *He's always focusing on his little traps and tricks, never working on what it really takes to catch a dragon: speed,* she thought to herself as she sprinted.

Ahead, the boy risked a glance over his shoulder. He spotted her, then sped off at a much faster pace.

Clara's legs practically flew over the ground, but the boy had a head start and the advantage of not being soaking wet.

BEEP! BEEEEEeeeeeeeeep!

Clara glanced to her left, and realized that there was a tar road cutting right through the forest. The occasional car lazily drove by, unaware of the chase mere yards away.

The boy, somehow always a step ahead, had clearly seen the road as well, and was veering towards it. She could calculate in her head that he would reach the road before she could quite easily, but that didn't mean she was giving up. She forced a boost of speed into her legs, now having lost all track of Mr. S somewhere in the woods behind her.

Clara came within shooting range, and she reached to pull her weapon out of a holder around her thigh. But to her dismay, her fingers closed in around empty air. *No!* She mentally roared. She must have dropped it when the car had run into the river. *If only S had let me have the wheel, we wouldn't have driven in and I would have my gun!*

But still she didn't relent. She pushed herself harder, the muscles in her legs burning. Her hair was wild around her in her falling-apart high ponytail, but she didn't care. The kid was clearly trying to time his run with a gray truck coming down the road. *The little toothpick is trying to hitchhike!*

The distance between herself and the kid was getting smaller and smaller, but the boy was closer to the truck. She put one final burst of energy into her legs, closing the distance to feet... to inches.... she reached out a hand to grab his shirt...

She felt a blast of wind blast past her as the gray truck zoomed by, and not a heartbeat later the child had hopped onto the back, clinging to the sides. "NOOOOO!" She screamed, the power in her legs failing as she slowed to an angry stop. "GET BACK HERE!"

But the boy only glanced back at her, looking quite terrified and even more winded. He clung to the side of the back of the truck like a lifeline. Clara could just barely make out the blue and green forms of two pocket dragons in his chest pocket.

So close, she had been *so close.*

She stood there breathing until Mr. S came sprinting up beside her, looking quite unaccustomed to running. "You lost them."

She shot him a glare. "You couldn't even keep up!"

Mr. S frowned, which was pretty much the only emotion she had ever seen him reveal.

"I told the Keeper not to have you come. You decided to burst your way in and assault that old man, giving the kid a warning. Then you don't listen to my shooting instructions, and take control of the car. Then you drive it into a river. Now you've chased the boy right onto a ride, leaving us in the middle of the woods. Literally."

Clara snorted, and buttoned up her suit jacket. "Are you listening to me?" Mr. S added. She continued to ignore him, then proceeded to stalk out into the middle of the road. "Clara, what are you doing?"

Clara pinned a stray hair behind her ear. She could hear the rumble of an engine down the road. She kept her attention straight ahead as she answered:

"I'm catching us a ride."

16
Survival

Isis gently set her talons on the shoulder and flank of a young dragonet. Blood as red as the young dragon's scales oozed from a gash on the side of the chest that the dragonet had gained upon his entry into the Glass Cage. Isis kindled her spark inside of her, felt its warmth in her core, then let it gurgle up through her throat and out of her open jaws. Shimmery golden fire bathed the wound of the dragonet, and slowly the wound closed under the healing magic in her fire. The pained expression on the young dragon melted away. "Your flesh is healed but the bone will require more time. Just rest here for a couple weeks. We will take care of you," she instructed.

The dragonet weakly nodded her head, her eyes still closed.

Isis gave a faint, sad smile and turned away, looking for another patient. Yet all the dragons in the alcove in the tree appeared to have already been tended to. There were dozens of dragons crammed into this recovery alcove alone, and there were many more packed with injured and healing dragons. The population inside the glass cage numbered in the thousands now, and they were already running out of room.

For despite the small size of the dragons and the general enormity of the Glass Cage, the dens and nooks inside the trees were sparse, meaning that most of the healthy dragons had to sleep on branches in full view of observing humans or worse, on the ground; a situation leaving many dragons feeling vulnerable and on edge. It also meant that sub-habitat space was limited.

Isis wandered over to the red fire crackling in the center of the room. This place was one of the many sub-habitats that she and Frida had arranged together. The elderly ice dragon from the south had been the first of many to require certain temperatures within the Glass Cage. Dragons originating from deserts of hot and cold needed certain temperatures in order to survive, and so the sub-habitats were created. Frida's fire was not an ordinary dragonflame— it was sparked out of raw magic, and was thus magic in itself.

Burning off nothing but Frida's own energy, it didn't devour the trees and plants. Thus, Frida could maintain a fire in every alcove, some cold and some hot, to accommodate for every dragon's needs. They couldn't have the fires out in the open lest the humans notice and take some precaution to inhibit their fire. Isis could hardly imagine the strain it must be putting on the meek dragoness, but she had insisted that she was used to it. That she had managed fires hundreds of times her own height for days on end. How a dragon could have such a magical capacity was truly incredible.

Isis peered into the crackling fire that danced with reds and yellows. The heat reminded her of the Egyptian sun... A warmth that she hadn't felt in...

It was hard to know how long anymore. She had so deeply embedded herself in her work trying to keep all of the dragons alive that she had just given up on keeping track.

They had also spent their time trying to study the humans— trying to figure out their motives. Isis had decided long ago that it wasn't plain human cruelty— so it had to be *some* reason, some cause. It wasn't uncommon for dragons to be caught only to be sold to humans as pets or to zoos or other worse fates. Yet why thousands of dragons were collected, brought into a massive Glass Cage out of public view... No one could understand it. Not even herself. Not even Frida.

Frida... She turned away from the warm fire and wandered over to the edge of the hole in the tree, and peered down at the central area of the cage. Frida was resting by the pool of water, nibbling on a food pellet. Every other day a cascade of hard, flavorless food pellets was thrown at them from the wind-tunnel. There was always exactly enough for every dragon to eat— though it was never quite enough for them to be completely full. It was hard enough dealing with the dragons who came in injured from the wind tunnel without having to quell scrabbles over food as well.

Ding dong.

The familiar sound rang inside the cage.

It sounded vaguely like a sound she had heard in an airport once, a sound that preceded some polite woman's voice asking someone to be somewhere or issuing boarding announcements.

Yet the voice that came after was most certainly not a polite woman's.

All the dragons currently awake and outside the alcoves turned their heads towards the metal doors that nearly blended in with the walls. A heartbeat later, they slid open, revealing none other than The Keeper.

He looked the same every time— square face, set jaw. He always reminded her of a general put in charge of a bunch of unwilling new recruits. If anything, he always sounded annoyed, as if the recruits had decided they wanted to become painters instead.

"Attention!" He commanded as he halted before them and took a square stance. "We are expecting visitors in exactly two hours. I expect you to behave, or there will be consequences." He glared at them. Without any further speech, he turned and strutted back out the sliding doors.

As soon as he had left, the dragons returned to their assorted activities. They hadn't had 'visitors' since that first time, which felt like a few weeks back. The keeper seemed to be trying to... Prove something to them... She recalled. Isis narrowed her eyes and peered down at Frida, who was now giving the rest of her food pellet to a young frost dragonet.

She felt the warm drafts from the fire that did not burn lick her back, then glanced once more at the sliding metal doors.

And began to formulate a plan.

17
Ice Cream and The Dragon Queen

Angus's stomach grumbled as he clung to the rim of William's chest pocket. He was really beginning to wish that he'd had time to eat some of the food the boy had presented them with earlier that day— the buttery, boiled potato sounded incredible just now. Angus was a fan of potatoes. Especially with melty sharp white cheddar cheese and salt and butter and—

"So why do you need to go to London?" William whispered, interrupting his thought process. Angus sank his claws deeper into the pocket fabric as they all jostled; they had been hitchhiking from lorries to busses to more conveyances, all in the direction of London, as per the dragon's instructions. Thankfully, William had obeyed their every word and had had very little time in between for questions.

Yet apparently their luck had ran out. Angus poked Azara in the side with a talon, who had been resting in the bottom of the pocket in order to rest her arm. She insisted it was fine, but Angus had argued that she needed not to aggravate it any further after the escape and chase.

Azara gave him a shrug, so Angus turned his head up and answered: "There is someone there who can help us." It was the best way to explain it that he could think of without mentioning the Dragon Queen. While humans knew very well of her existence, her exact location was a closely guarded secret among dragons.

William cocked his head as he looked down at them, his piercing green eyes curious yet afraid. "Help.... About those people who came for us?"

Angus nodded. "Yes."

The boy bit his lip in thought, then asked: "So why did they come for you? Why are they after you? Why not any other dragons?"

Angus and Azara exchanged another glance, and Azara and answered: "Those people... They had captured us, taken us against our will. We escaped... And now it seems they want us back." Azara cast her eyes to the side in contemplation. "Why... We still don't entirely know."

William looked thoughtful for a moment, then suddenly he lit up. "Your names! You never told me your names. Do you have names?" He asked excitedly.

Angus smiled. That was something he was comfortable talking about. "I'm Angus."

Azara looked a little more reluctant, but seemed to decide to relent. "Azara."

William smiled. "Angus.... Azara.... Those are brilliant names."

A sudden jolt made Angus glance around again, as did William. Buildings were appearing around them, and he realized that they must be entering London. He knew exactly where they needed to go... It was now just a matter of getting there without betraying the location to William.

For all dragons knew of the place of the Dragon Queen. It was taught to dragonets like 999 or 911 was taught to human children. For in a few ways, that's what she was.

The queen was more than just a queen- she was an ambassador. The lone dragon elected by both human and dragon kind, to be a voice, a bridge between the two. She was the only dragon who, by a law older than the Magna Carta, was granted an equal voice among humans. No matter what country, she was guaranteed all of the rights of any humans.

No human could rob her then say it was like taking a fish from a cat— that she had no voice.

Azara climbed up to the rim of the pocket and this time Angus didn't stop her. "Alright, so any brilliant plans for getting to the Parliament Building without leading Will right to it?" The blue dragoness asked.

"Hmmm..." Angus thought. "Well... Firstly, do you know how to get there in the first place?"

"Well of course!" She answered like it was nothing at all. "I grew up in London, I could get anywhere with my eyes closed." She spoke as if it were a plain fact. "We just need to find a way to shake off the boy now that he's gotten us the bulk of the way."

And soon, Angus realized as he glanced around at their surroundings again. *We're already in London.*

Angus opened his mouth to respond, but the sudden jolt as the truck went over another bump had him briefly interrupted. Yet before he could finally answer, William said: "Guys, it's them! They've found us!" He whispered urgently.

Angus climbed up William's red shirt and onto his shoulder so that he could see behind them.

There, speeding towards them, was the insane woman who had been shooting at them back in the woods around Willough. No helmet guarded her head as her black hair flew wild about her. For she was riding....

"Where did she get a motorcycle!" Azara exclaimed as she joined him on the boy's shoulder. Angus then remembered that there had been two of them, and his eyes led him to a familiar form riding in...

A sidecar?

The man didn't look all too happy about it either, squished into a little sidecar out of his control.

What Angus wasn't happy about was the shiny metal black thing that the man was now pulling out of an inside jacket pocket.

"William, DUCK!" Angus commanded as he flattened himself on the boy's shoulder. Will bent down to hide beneath the sides of the back of the truck.

And not a moment too soon. BANGPOP! The sound of a gun firing went off swiftly followed by a dangerous jolt of the truck— and not from going over a bump. Then there was the sound of metal scraping on tarmac at a high speed— not a pleasant sound.

"WHO'S SHOOT'N AT ME TRUCK?" The driver bellowed.

BANGPOP! Was the answer.

The truck made another dangerous lurch as suddenly the sound of metal on tarmac was doubled and they were suddenly at an angle.

"The wheels have been shot!" William burst in realization, and poked his head over the side.

"He's trying to get us grounded!" Angus added. "We need to get off now, while he's focusing on the wheels!" He instructed.

The truck was indeed dramatically slowing down, and the motorcycle and sidecar was a dangerous couple feet behind them. This street of London was relatively empty of both cars and pedestrians, leaving no one to witness their plight. "Get off, William. While the roads are empty! We can run for it!" Angus urged again.

Angus dug his claws in as William readied himself, then vaulted over the side of the truck. The boy immediately made a break for the sidewalk.

BANG! BANG! BANG!

Bullets whizzed past them and left bullet holes embedded in nearby buildings. William kept running and took off down the sidewalk.

The growl of the motorcycle's engine sounded behind them. Angus glanced behind him to see the woman driving the motorcycle and sidecar dangerously close to the sidewalk and right towards them.

"Turn this way, Will!" Azara shouted, pointing wildly with a talon towards a narrow alley sharp to their right.

Angus continued watching their pursuers as William veered towards the alley. "Sorry Mr. S," The woman said as she began to swerve towards the alley. She leaned over dangerously and yanked out a bolt that had been connecting the sidecar to the motorcycle. "But I can't have you slowing me up."

"Clara! Clara no!" Mr. S yelled.

Alas, it was too late. The sidecar went wheeling past down the road, containing a very exasperated looking Mr. S, and Clara made the sharp turn down the alley.

"Hurry, Wills!" Angus urged as the woman sped towards them. Angus watched as she came closer and closer....

The alley broke out into open road, and William dodged to the side, not two seconds before Clara sped past. "Go left!" Azara suddenly called. William obeyed and sped that way down the street. The road was crowded with people both walking and driving, and Will had to dive and weave between the river of humans.

Behind them, the motorcycle veered around, but was met with crowds of people, causing her to halt. She rapidly scanned around, and Angus was about to tell William to duck down and hide inside the crowd, but—

"Stop!" She had seen them "Thief! Stop that kid! He's trying to kidnap dragons!" She yelled, pointing an accusatory finger towards them as they ran away.

Suddenly, the crowd shifted from a protective force to a malicious mob.

It took a moment for the crowd to register Clara's yelling, giving Will enough time to bolt through them. Hands reached for them, trying to snag them...

"Turn right!" Azara commanded. William veered through the grabbing crowds in the ordered direction. Yet suddenly there was a parting in the humans around them, along with the roaring of an engine...

Clara was speeding through the crowds down the sidewalk, not stopping for anyone, leaving the people to wildly jump out of her path. William ran down the road, though in his rapid running he began to sag.

"Hop on that bus!" Azara suddenly ordered, pointing with a talon to a double-decker tour bus about to turn a corner onto another street.

"What?" William questioned, his voice ragged from exertion.

"Just hop it!" She yelled firmly.

And so the boy sprinted straight for the back of the bus and jumped for it; he grabbed the bars on the back and clung to them. The unknowing bus turned the corner, and Clara once again overshot them in her speed and went zooming down in the wrong direction.

"Now what?!" William asked.

Azara climbed back onto his shoulder from where she had slid onto his back in the chase. Angus momentarily felt bad at how many scratches the poor boy must be getting underneath his shirt from all of the dragon's clinging to him.

The blue dragoness scanned around, taking in the surroundings and identifying where they were. "The place we need to be is just a few blocks from here. Just keep following my instructions and—"

PLOP!

Angus slowly turned his head to the white, wet blob slowly sliding down the back of the bus, a few inches from his face. With a....

Cone sticking out?

He turned his head around to see behind them, and saw not a motorcycle but an...

Ice cream truck?

Indeed, wildly swerving towards them through the London traffic, was Mr. S in an ice cream truck...

With Clara careening half out an open window, looking very much ready to lob a bunch of chocolate and vanilla ice creams at them.

The tour bus made another turn, briefly bringing them out of range. "HOW THE BLAZES DID THEY GET AN ICE CREAM TRUCK!" Will yelled.

Angus peered behind them again. "I don't know, but WATCH OUT FOR—"

PLOPOP!

A barrage of ice cream crashed into the back of the bus around them.

Angus poked a talon into the mysterious pink ice cream splattered right next to him, then brought it to his mouth and licked it. He then turned to the truck wildly weaving towards them and bellowed. "HEY! THIS ICE CREAM IS TERRIBLE! I THINK THE CREAM

WAS SOUR! THOUGH MAYBE THAT WAS JUST YOU! REMIND ME NEVER TO GET ICE CREAM FROM YOU AGAIN!"

They were answered by another cold, creamy assault; one ice cream landing square on William's back. "Gah!" He complained.

At this, Angus made another jeer towards the ice cream truck. "HEY! I GET THE WHOLE MOVING THE MERCHANDISE THING, BUT THIS IS JUST OVERDOING IT! VERY BAD REVIEW COMING YOUR WAY!"

He then felt a jab in the shoulder. "Angus!" Azara growled. "Stop aggravating them!"

Angus opened his snout to reply, yet before he could—

They were both covered in wet, cold creaminess.

The blobs of ice cream being considerably larger than them, the impact was surprisingly forceful. Before Angus could even realize it, he was plastered to the bus wall in a soft-serve, sprinkle, caramel mess, with only his head poking out. Azara was in a similar unfortunate situation beside him.

Angus felt himself slowly slide down the bus, slowly towards that black road racing underneath... He tried to struggle free but caramel was a surprisingly strong-gripped adversary. He managed to burst a talon free, but he was sliding too fast... *Of all things.... Death by ice cream... Why couldn't it have at least been death by sheep? That would have at least been fluffy... Oh no—!*

Fingers closed around him and pulled him from the sticky sweet disaster. They quickly set him down on William's shoulder, then the boy reached for Azara.

"Thanks mate," Azara panted as she was set down beside Angus.

"Don't thank me yet!" William interjected. "Where do we need to go now?"

"Errrrrrrrmmmmmmmm....." Azara quickly looked around. "Straight!"

William glanced at the taillights of the bus. They blinked indicating left. "I'm going to have to jump as it's turning the corner," he explained, and braced for the jump.

"Sounds good to me!" Angus agreed. Behind them, the ice cream truck was madly maneuvering through traffic towards them, the giant pink ice cream cone on top dangerously careening this way and that. Angus dived into the boy's pocket to secure for the jump, and Azara was right behind him.

The bus began to turn, revealing the street ahead... The parliament building, with the sunlight bouncing off its brilliant bronze tower, lay just ahead. "Big Ben," Angus breathed.

And William jumped.

He landed on the road, and rolled. Cars jolted to a halt around them and let out many furious honks, yet miraculously he was not hit as he barrel rolled along the ground then jumped to his feet in the middle of the intersection.

"Come on!" Azara urged, and William set off running again, dodging between the halted cars until he reached the sidewalk.

Miraculously, he managed not to be hit by any vehicle.

Yet that ice cream truck is.... Still a concern. Angus thought. Indeed, the ice cream truck was still rapidly making for them... And Clara was still lobbing various ice creams at them, many of which were now splattering on nearby cars. The woman had moved on to full gallons now, which crashed into car doors and windows with considerable impact— causing several unfortunate windows to shatter.

"Go towards the Parliament building!" Azara yelled.

William sprinted like mad for the ordered location, his legs flying beneath him. Gallons of ice cream whizzed passed them, many hitting several unlucky pedestrians. They were so close.... Just a few dozen more feet...

Then suddenly, Angus watched in horror as a gallon of mint chocolate chip connected right with the back of William's head.

And the boy started falling for the pavement. "RuN ANg..azra..." His voice became steadily more groggy as he fell.

Angus spread his ice cream-covered wings and leapt off into the sky, beating the air furiously

Plop.

Will hit the ground.

Angus wanted to turn and make sure he was alright, but Azara flew past him and called: "Come on! He'll be fine!"

Angus bit his lip to keep himself from looking back, and churned the air harder under his wings and sped up. The mad ice cream truck ignored William conked out on the ground and now zoomed straight towards them— and Clara was chucking various ice cream bars at them at high speed.

"Just a bit further! It's right through there!" Azara yelled, pointing towards a little, pocket dragon sized door right above the clock of the tower. Angus angled his wings, flapping harder and harder to go higher and higher... Ice cream splats were beginning to decorate the clock tower....

By now Angus could see the details on the golden little doors, the swirling designs of pocket dragons beautifully depicted all over the doors.

And then he collided right into them.

And then crashed right through them as they were blown open from the impact.

Angus collapsed onto the bronze ground. "Ughhhhh..." He moaned. He didn't even want to open his eyes; he just wanted to take a nice, long nap... Dream about sleeping on sheep, and not being chased by a pair of mad, ice cream-lobbing agents....

"Angus..." Azara whispered, lying on the ground beside him. "Angus, get up..."

Reluctantly, he opened his eyes.

"Oh."

He looked around in sudden awe at the circular pocket dragon sized throne room around them. Elegant bronze wood walls rose around them in a pyramid, and seats perfectly fitted for pocket dragons circled them like in a stadium. A magnificent diamond chandelier burning dragonflame lit up the entire room. Beautiful carpets of blue, green and red with golden embroidery of dragons covered the floor. At the very front, a majestic golden throne set with shining jewels stood empty.

And surrounding them, were dozens upon dozens of dragons.

The Dragon Court, Angus suddenly realized as he slowly pushed himself to his talons. *And from the looks of it, we've just interrupted something very, very important...*

"Halt!" A dragon suddenly commanded, and Angus turned to see a set of emerald green guard dragons beginning to circle them. They carried spears with sharp metal tips... Tips now pointed at them. "You there!" A prominent dragon in silver armor commanded, pointing his spear at Angus's snout. "Are you responsible for what's happened to the queen?"

Angus threw up his talons in innocence, and prayed that Azara wouldn't retort some feisty snap at the guards. "Please! We have come with urgent news!" He pleaded.

The guard in silver armor poked his cheek with the spear. "Do you have anything to do with the queen?"

Angus twitched his ear, suddenly hearing what the guard was saying. "What happened to the queen? Please, we must speak with her, we have critical information." He looked around desperately at the rings of dragons encircling them.

The guards all took a moment exchanging looks, and concern built up in Angus's chest.

Finally, a guard in golden armor stepped forward. "You mean you really do not know?"

Angus shook his head. "No, I don't, I promise. What happened?!"

The dragon in silver took a breath, then looked him in the eye. "The Queen is missing," he said.

"And we suspect she's been kidnapped.

18
A Story of Storm and Fire

"What!?" Frida meekly exclaimed.

Isis kept her gaze and voice calm but pleading. "Frida, this is our *best* chance, and *you're* the *only* one who can do what we need. You are the final piece of the puzzle to our escape."

Frida nervously shook her head and inched backwards a step. "But... I... What if I fail..."

Isis sat down and curled her tail over her talons. "You won't fail, Frida. I've seen what you can do, and I know that you can do this."

"Besides," a silvery dragon said as she flapped down out of the sky and landed besides Isis. "If you fail, then we'll just keep going. Your fire won't hurt us, so it's not like we'd die if the plan backfires," Iah pointed out.

Frida's shoulders slumped, her wings crumpled around her. "But... I've never done anything like this before.... What if I can't make it convincing enough? What if they see right through it and punish us instead?"

Isis twitched her tail and rose again to her talons. "There isn't time to worry. This will either work or it won't, and all the dragons have already been informed of the plan. We have likely only a few minutes till those humans come back." Isis fixed her in her queenly look. "Frida, please, you *must* do this. For all of us here in the Glass Cage. For maybe even all of Pocket Dragon kind."

Frida opened her jaw and was about to object again, when the whirring noise suddenly sounded from overhead. They turned their heads up to watch as the wind-tunnel opened, and dragons began plummeting through and down into the cage. One hundred dragons rained down, and as soon as the last one was through, the tunnel snapped shut with deadly speed.

The new arrivals groaned on the ground, and many dragons rushed to help them, Frida included. Glad to escape from Isis and Iah's pleadings, she busied herself trying to help a white dragoness to her talons. "Are you alright?" She asked.

"I... I think I went a little deeper than anticipated on my quest," the dragoness answered, lifting her head to meet her gaze.

Frida froze at the sight of her. At the brilliant, pearly, luminescent white scales, tinted with frosty blue. At the long, swirling, curving, elegant white horns tinted with lilac.

At the white chestplates with swirling silver designs. At the lovely lilac and silver wings. At the delicate yet powerful frame.

At her striking eyes.

They were a faded cobalt blue with little silver specks.

Like looking at a sapphire in a blizzard.

The dragoness before her had briefly frozen as well, but quickly came back to herself. "I'm sorry. Do you know where we are?" She asked politely.

Isis was suddenly at Frida's side, perhaps to check that everything was all right, and suddenly halted. Then bowed. The Goddess of the Sun, *bowed.* "Your Majesty!"

Ice shot down Frida's spine as she sank into a bow as well. *Queen. I was talking to the queen. I was talking to the queen and I didn't even know it. Is she mad at me for not bowing immediately? How was she captured? If the Dragon Queen is here, does that mean that it's already too late to save dragon kind?* Her mind raced.

"Please, rise," the Dragon Queen said. "I do not believe that this is the time for posturing and formalities."

"Thank you, my Queen." Isis rose from her bow. "Indeed, time is critical. We are just about to lodge another escape attempt and—"

The sound of sliding metal screeched behind them, and every dragon turned towards the metal doors sliding open.

The Keeper strolled in first, once again wearing his usual garb and shades despite the fact that they were indoors. Following him came the four leaders that they had seen last time, all wearing similar attire from their previous encounter.

"Where is your boss this time, Mr. K?" The tall gaunt man asked as they came to a stop around the Glass Cage. "You assured us that they would be here today. Or are they still off on... Business?"

The Keeper hardly reacted. "They will be here in just a few minutes, sir. Their flight was delayed." The man nodded towards to the cage. "But meanwhile, I invite you to notice that we are now at half capacity, and the dragons are thriving."

The leaders took a step closer to the cage to inspect it.

A gentle brush on her wing made her snap her head in the direction of the touch. There stood Isis, her emerald eyes intent with one word.

Now.

Frida flitted her eyes back to the humans peering in at them with stone faces, but their words were mere jumbles to her now. She could already feel her spark burning within her, urging her on.

Her magic surged through her like pulsing waves as she built up a larger spark inside her core. There was no room for failure— if she didn't pull this off, who knows when their next escape chance would be— if ever. She tried to quell the rising thoughts of fear that wanted to cloud her mind... *All these dragons are relying on me... I can't do it... I've never done this before... What if I fail....* She forced those thoughts away and replaced them with those of Siberia. Of the cozy nights curled up on Kostya's lap or shoulder or knee in front of the gentle fire as her guardian told her stories late into the night. Of the long hours watching Kostya read his stories and sometimes write a few of his own. Whenever he finished them he would go sprinting out into the snow to look for her, call her name with such happiness on his old face, and have her come to listen to them.

There was one story that he hadn't finished yet before she had been captured. He never even let her peek a glance at it, and she had curiously waited for him to finish it, wondering what the mysterious secret story was and why he guarded it so closely.

If we don't escape... If I can't free us... Then I might never hear Kostya's story.

With that thought powering her, she dropped open her jaws and let great white fire come cascading out.

This fire wasn't a gentle bath or a calm hearth fire— it was a flood. It swept through the cage as if a dam had broken, engulfing everything in its path with completely harmless flame.

Yet the cries of pain and agony were still remarkably convincing. *It's just acting... I'm not burning anyone...* She told herself and forced herself to keep bellowing out great churning fires. By now her flame appeared to have consumed over half of the Glass Cage.

She heard thuds as dragons desperately threw themselves against the glass, wailing in mock agony. *All part of the plan... All part of the plan...* She reminded herself. She willed her fire to climb up the trees as if out of control, to rage like a wildfire. She saw a cluster of dragons pressing themselves against the glass in desperation, and had a wave of fire crash over them just for dramatics. They screamed quite realistically as they were 'drowned' by the fire and 'devoured'.

It took all of her focus to maintain this much fire, to manage the temperature so that it was harmless, and to keep the fire growing. She quickly began to feel drained, but she knew that if she stopped now, the plan would fail.

She cast a glance towards the humans outside the cage. The roar of her fire and the screams of the dragons made it hard to hear their words, but it appeared that they were arguing. A couple of the leaders seemed to be outright yelling at the keeper and pointing at the cage. The keeper made a few gestures towards the cage as well, but one of the leaders who had been yelling made a final step forward, said something, and the exasperated keeper stormed over to a wall and flipped open a metal panel.

Beneath it were a series of flashing buttons, and the keeper jabbed one of them with a pudgy finger, and suddenly an alarm went off.

And the Glass Cage began to open.

The two halves of the massive cylinder slid around, opening a massive gaping way out.

The dragons rushed through it like a flood.

It was a storm of multi-colored scales as hundreds of dragons rushed through the opening gap. Frida finally snapped her jaw closed, cutting off her fire yet still letting it pretend to burn up the inside of the cage. The rush of dragons above her was so thick, like a torrential storm, and she was intimidated to jump into it, afraid she might be knocked out of the sky or caught again by one of the people in suits...

She felt a brush on her wing again. Isis was still standing there, just as she had been, and giving her another look. But this time she could afford words. "Let's go."

Fear thudded in her heart, but Frida nodded.

And spread her wings.

And leapt into the storm of dragons and fire.

She lost all track of Isis and the queen in the frenzy, and it was all she could to keep flying with the dragons and not get thrown out of the sky by a stray wing or leg or tail. The wave of dragons almost acted as one— as one, massive dragon, like the dragons of old. They surged towards the metal door to where the leaders were fleeing. The keeper was trying to pull them back, but the business people continued to flee the mob of dragons and ran towards the doors.

The doors opened, and the dragons rushed through.

Steel walls rushed passed them as they sped down the corridor, rushing for anything that might be an exit. Scales and talons and horns flashed by her as they veered left and right in completely and utterly random directions.

They sped around one corner to find a pair of men in suits running towards them with a net, and so the dragons instantly whirled around and flew down in the other direction. Around another corner they found a hall with nothing but a disturbing obsidian-black door at the end.

Then they turned yet another corner of the steel labyrinth, and there they saw it: A door. Yet not just any door— unlike any of the other mysterious doors they had flown past, this one has a label printed over it.

Dragon Shop it read.

And a shop could only mean one thing:

A way out.

The dragons swarmed like bees towards that door, which also unlike the others doors, had a simple handle in place of a keypad. A trio of dragons pulled down the handle, and under the force of dozens of dragons ramming into it, blasted the door open.

Frida zoomed through the door and past a very confused-looking blue-shirted man. She only got brief glimpses at the room around her— but it was enough to tell that it was most definitely a pet shop. Cages of varying sizes lines the walls and tables, all full of dragons.

Frida paused mid air, letting the rush of dragons fly past her as she stared at the cages, at the hopeless dragons inside them.... *There has got to be some way to free them, too...*

She tilted her wings to dive towards them, when she felt talons close around her tail. They released her when she whipped around to see who it was, and silver scales greeted her. "We haven't time to rescue them now! Once we have escaped, we can put a stop to this!" Iah insisted.

Frida cast a reluctant glance at the Moon Goddess and looked back down at the caged dragons. *She's probably right... But how can we just leave them here? What if something happens?* Yet before she could voice her concerns, Isis was by her side.

"Come on! There's no time to waste! They'll be fine!" She urged. With that, Frida finally relented and dived back into a swift flight towards the double doors at the pet shop entrance....

The storm of dragons slammed into the doors, blowing them open, and the dragons flew out into the open air.

Into freedom.

19
Time and Tornadoes

"Kidnapped?" Azara exclaimed. "How does the queen - *the* Dragon Queen, get kidnapped? Doesn't she have guards? Where was she? When was the last you saw her?"

The guard shook his head in dismay. "She does— usually."

Azara raised a brow. "Usually?"

The guard sighed. "There was a dragon robbing the treasury. We all left to apprehend him, and when we returned.... She was gone." He explained.

Azara bit her lip in thought. "So you think she was taken while you were gone?" She asked, taking a surveying glance around the court. "But... Wouldn't there have been witnesses?" She pointed out, indicating with a wing to the Dragon Court. "And uh, a gaping hole in the wall?" She added.

The guard shook his head. "No— she left of her own free will, that we are sure of."

"What?" She asked. "How do you know?"

A mint green dragon stepped forward from his seat in the front row. He was old, judging by his long twisted horns, and he wore a pair of tiny glasses over his snout. "We did not see her leave. She likely used the commotion of the guards rushing out to sneak out."

Azara furrowed her brows confusedly. "But... Why would she want to sneak out?"

The guard and the elderly dragon exchanged a look, and finally the latter answered: "Despite her best intentions to hide it from us, the queen had been on a... Quest of sorts for the past few seasons. She disappears now and again, but until now, she has managed to return unscathed and usually before we even noticed. But the queen has been gone for a few hours now since the robbery."

Beside her, Angus cocked his head. "What sort of quest? Like, the quest for the Golden Sheep?"

The guard shook his head. "Not quite—"

Suddenly there was a *slam!* As the doors blew open and a lilac guard dragoness came sliding to a halt in the middle of the room. She immediately turned her head to the guard who they were speaking to, her sides heaving from exertion. "Sir, you must come outside. There is something you need to see. Right now," she panted urgently.

The guard and several others then proceeded to race down the hall, and Azara joined in after them, just as curious as to what might be going on outside. The guards all leapt right out of the golden-bronze door and into the air, while Azara skidded to a halt right at the edge. Angus was right beside her as she craned her neck out to see...

A tornado?

No... Azara thought, narrowing her eyes and the strange swirling spiral off in the distance, just a couple blocks away. *A swarm?...* She steadied her grip and narrowed her eyes further. *No... Not a swarm... Not a tornado...*

Dragons.

A great swirling mass of scales and wings spiraled up towards the sky, indeed looking quite like what she had initially thought it to be. Yet it was, in fact, a tornado of dragons—hundreds upon hundreds of dragons all fleeing into the sky.

Fleeing... Definitely fleeing... She judged, based on the speed and great quantity, *but from what?*

Yet the origin of their escape was cloaked behind the rooftops of other buildings. *I have to get closer,* she decided, and jumped off from the little doorway and into the air.

"Azara!" Angus called from the ledge behind her. "Azara!"

Azara glanced over her shoulder back at him, but continued to fly away. "I have to see where they are coming from!" She called back to him.

"Azara!" Angus persisted, but finally he gave in and jumped into the air, frantically flapping after her. "Shouldn't we leave this to the guards or something?"

This time, Azara didn't look back. "If you haven't noticed, they were sort of busy dealing with him," she said, flicking her tail to indicate to the ground where a pale blue dragon was racing across the bridge lugging a sack of presumably treasure. The guards were indeed occupied in the chase.

"Hmph," Angus muttered behind her. "Really what is the point of those guys if they go off chasing squirrels whenever something vastly more important is going on?"

Azara grinned just a slight. "I suppose that's why we're here then!" And without any further conversation, she dived down into a soft glide towards the dragon tornado.

As she drew closer, the tornado began to disperse as dragons went darting away in various and seemingly random directions. Yet there was still a flow of dragons surging from what appeared to be a shattered storefront. Azara tilted her wings for more speed as she glided down towards the scene.

Her talons set down on cold road a bit away from the storefront. The mass of dragons escaping was now thinning, with only a few stragglers now flying through. The last one appeared to be a white dragon helping to carry what seemed to be an injured dragonet. The white dragoness landed on the ground near the storefront instead of shooting off into the sky—likely over-weighted by the young dragon.

Crash! Glass went flying everywhere as a trio of people in black suits jumped through what remained of the storefront; any glass remaining was blown away completely. Not a moment later they had the straggling white dragon and dragonet surrounded in a triangle formation. The two humans directly facing the dragons had pistols trained on them, whereas the man behind him was pulling a dark sack out of his inside jacket pocket.

It was all happening too fast— those last dragons would be caught in seconds and there were no witnesses and no one to help and—

"Stop!" A strong Irish voice commanded from behind her. She whipped around to see Angus standing with a talon outreached towards the unfolding scene.

Azara whirled back towards the scene to see if his warning had worked.

They had, indeed, stopped.

Azara cocked her head and furrowed her brow. The scene hadn't just stopped, it had frozen. Not even the dragon's or human's sides heaved with breath. It was completely, utterly still.

It was as if time had stopped.

She slowly turned back towards Angus, who held his talon outstretched. "Angus...?"

His eyes flicked between her and the frozen scene, and finally he said: "Go! Get help. And hurry!"

Azara hesitated for a moment, a million questions racing through her mind, but after a "Now!" From Angus, she put aside her questions and jumped into the sky, furiously beating her wings. Below her, the three dark-suited humans and pair of dragons remained absolutely, impossibly still.

She turned her attention away from the montage beneath and soared off looking for help. She scanned over the nearby roads, when she spotted a circle of policemen surrounding a cluster of dragons atop a circular table. *Perfect,* she thought, and descended right towards the middle.

Standing in front of the cluster, a golden dragon appeared to be trying to speak with the police, desperately trying to get them to listen. She seemed... Familiar, somehow. When she was within landing distance, she suddenly recognized her. *The golden dragon from the lab.... The same one who helped us escape!* She realized. *She sent us off to free the captured dragons... Yet it appears that she got them out herself,* she thought with a flicker of shame.

She landed on the table with a light click of her talons on the metal. The golden dragon turned from her apparent arguing and seemed to recognize her. "How are you here? What happened? Were you able to escape? I had hoped, since we never saw you in the Glass Cage..."

Azara bit back her answers, her apologies for failing them, and focused on the immediate task at talon. "I'll explain later. Right now, there's a dragon in danger of being caught again— there were three of those awful people surrounding them. My friend has sort of got them..." She racked her brains for a way to describe it. "Frozen in action." Her voice turned to a whisper to assure that the police didn't hear. "If we can get the police to come and catch them in the act..." She hinted.

The golden dragon smiled. "Then it's perfect evidence to prove to them that what's happening is real."

Azara nodded and grinned, then turned to the police and jumped into the sky, hovering before them. "Please, you must help!" She cried to the humans, drawing out all of her acting skills to appear dramatic. "Someone is in danger! I saw them being chased by these horrible people with guns and one of them had a sack! You *must* come quickly, I fear they may be *killed*!" She turned in the air and started flapping down an alley towards the storefront.

"Come, you must hurry!" She called back, giving them no time for questions.

To her relief, she heard the thunder of racing boots behind her. She had caught their attention all right. *Now all that's left is to get them to the men in dark suits... If it isn't too late.*

She gave a few powerful strokes of her wings to boost her speed, thinking of what chaos might have erupted since she had left.

Come on Angus; just hold on a little longer, she mentally urged.

I'm coming!

20

Justice Among Dragons and Men

"Halt!" A policeman ordered as they skidded into the street outside a shattered storefront. Glass littered the narrow walking road, and three men surrounded a white dragoness and a dragonet on the ground just outside the storefront.

It's the queen, Isis realized in horror. The scene before them suddenly started into motion— a man with a sack swung it down towards the queen as the two with guns kept them distracted. "Stop!" A policeman ordered again. The three men in suits looked startled and finally noticed the cops. They were disoriented enough that the cops managed to surround them before they seemed to even fully see what was happening. "You are all under arrest for attempted capture of a dragon."

Isis didn't bother to watch the rest of the human's interactions, and instantly rushed for the queen. The royal also seemed rather disoriented by the sudden appearance of the police, yet relieved. "Are you alright, your Majesty?" Isis asked. Beside her the blue dragoness that had informed her of the situation went straight to the dragonet by the queen and carried him safely away to a group of dragons collecting on a rooftop nearby.

The white dragoness lifted herself to her talons. "Yes, miraculously yes. Thank you," she answered, remarkably collected considering her close call. Isis led her safely away from where the police were handcuffing the men in black suits, over to the corner of the alley near a potted fern. "And well done," The queen added. "It was a brilliant plan. I must thank you as well for rescuing me..."

"Isis Bastet, of the Egyptians. Yet the humans like to call me their Goddess of the Sun." Isis smiled but shook her head. "I cannot be to thank for all of the work. My friend Frida was the one who pulled it off— if it hadn't been for her, we would still be in that cage." Isis twisted around, looking for the aforementioned dragoness. Alas, she was nowhere to be seen. *Must have taken off after the escape,* she hoped. *I'll find her later,* she decided and turned back to the queen.

"Yes, I would like to speak with her, actually, next time you find her," the queen said with a distracted expression. Then she refocused, those striking, smart eyes meeting her own glittering green ones. Both queens in their own right, both respecting each other as such. "Yet right now, we need to deal with these people. What has happened to these dragons is unacceptable— we need to do something about it."

Isis nodded. "Most definitely." She subtly flexed her wings in thought, tired from the mad flight after weeks of confinement. Suddenly an idea occurred to her. "My queen, may I suggest a trial?" She offered.

The queen slowly raised a brow in consideration. "That is an idea.... The humans do like having things on their terms. If we had a trial and proved that what happened to the dragons was real and wrong..."

Isis cracked a slight grin. "... Then they would have no choice but to acknowledge it and end it for good," she finished.

The queen nodded, revealing a slight grin of her own. "Brilliant," she said decidedly, taking a step back and angling her wings for flight. "I shall arrange for a trial. With any luck I shall be seeing you soon, Isis Bastet of the Egyptians."

Isis bowed her head. "Thank you, your majesty," she said, watching as the elegant dragon soared off into the sky.

A trial it is, then... She thought.

Let's make things right.

21

Sheep in the Courtroom

Angus paced back and forth on the little ledge of wood on the wall of the waiting room. *Why did I agree to this?* He thought. *Why in the woolly world of sheep would I agree to this?* He self reprimanded. *I don't know the first thing about giving a testimony or argument or whatever the legal term for this is...*

"Calm down," Azara snapped, sitting on the top of a massive cushy maroon armchair. "You are going to be fine. All we need to do is convince the judge that what happened was real, then they can shut down the whole operation!" She said. "Seriously, after all we've been through, having been *captured* by an *evil lab, chased* all over Britain by a pair of creepy *people in suits,* and almost *killed* by *ice cream*— I would think that this would be a flight with the wind to you."

Angus flung up his foretalons in exasperation. "But, what if I say the wrong thing? What if I look suspicious then *I'm* put on trial? For like, some sheep thievery or something? Aren't dragons always accused of stealing sheep? Even though we are a fraction of the size of them?!"

Azara flapped up and joined him on the ledge, forcing him to halt his pacing on the narrow space. "Stop worrying. You will be fine! Just be sure to mention the fact that they captured us against our will, sold us, and shot at us— especially that first and last part."

Angus slowly nodded his head, trying to calm down. "Yes... Yes... Then Frida will talk about what happened inside the lab..."

Sitting on the edge of the little round wooden table by the armchair, the shy icy dragon nodded. "I will explain our experience and how we were kept there and treated," she said, her meek voice hardly audible across the room. "About how we were treated as... Mere animals."

Angus was about to plunge back into the vortex of mortal terror about the trial, when the doors suddenly whooshed open. Through them glided in the golden dragon, who had introduced herself as Isis when she found himself and Azara and told them about the trial. Gliding in behind her came the elderly mint green dragon whom they had spoken to back at the Dragon Court.

"Are you all prepared?" Isis asked promptly, hovering above them. "Well, we have to be in just a couple minutes regardless," she said without giving them a chance to answer. She nodded towards her green companion and said: "This is Eoghan, a trusted member of the Dragon Court. The queen herself assigned him to us. He will be acting as your lawyer," she introduced. "Eoghan, meet Frida, Angus, and Azara."

The green dragon nodded. "It is a pleasure to meet you all," he said, and adjusted his spectacles with a talon as he said: "Now, I wish I'd had the time to speak with you before the trial, but the humans insisted on today or next year due to their *busy* schedules, and so logically we had to settle for today. Isis and the queen filled me in to their best ability beforehand, so hopefully I'll have enough information to see us through this."

Again Angus was about to open his mouth to let out the flood of questions, yet once more the opening of the doors interrupted him. This time a human head poked through. "It's time," he said simply before disappearing again back out through the doors.

Angus gulped, ice crystallizing in his belly. His talons felt like they were turning to stone.

Then a different set of talons rested on his shoulder, and he turned to see Azara beside him. Her shimmery silver eyes seemed to emit a feeling of calm and reassurance. "Let's go," she said.

No no no no no this is a bad idea I'm going to do terribly I'm going to fail everyone and "Alright," his mouth said. *Bad mouth! Baaaad baaaad mouth!* He mentally growled at himself. *Why did I say that I should have said I was dying or something—*

Azara jumped into the air and began flapping towards the door. Angus half jumped-half-fell into the air after her. *No wings! Listen to me!* He commanded, but for some reason he was following her. He felt like he was in a daze.

They all flew out through the doors and down a corridor, following the man who had informed them it was time to enter. Angus let himself become distracted by the repeating pattern of golden thread on the red carpet beneath them as he flew above it, and was startled when Azara slowed down to glide beside him and asked in a hushed voice: "Do you want to tell me?"

"Huh?" He said confusedly, eyes widening.

Azara's expression remained gentle and curious. "About your magic. You told me at Willough that you had no magic, but..." She bit her lip as she considered her phrasing. "Why didn't you want to tell me? Why keep it a secret?"

"Oh..." His voice lowered as well and he moved to glide closer to her so that the others wouldn't hear. "My magic... it's... complicated," he explained. "Time is not something to be played with, nor messed with lightly." He took a steadying breath before continuing. "And... I feel like if I told anyone... They would want to use it. They would want me to change the past or future for their own benefit. In truth that's not exactly how this magic works... But, I feel it's best if as few people knew about it as possible. That way... That way it can't be misused." His little heart thumped in his chest.

But Azara only gave a solemn nod and the slightest of smiles. "I won't tell anyone. Your secret is safe with me," she assured.

Angus had the strangest sensation of a weight being lifted from his chest, leaving him feeling lighter. He hadn't even realized it was there until now, but having someone know... It felt... Better, somehow.

Then they reached the courtroom doors, and the relieved space was suddenly refilled with lead.

The human pushed the doors open, and they glided into the courtroom.

Angus was briefly distracted from his terror in fascination with the room. Mahogany wood walls gilded with gold rose around them, with cobblestone corners. Stained glass windows let multicolored light flood into the room, portraying pretty patterns over the red-carpeted floor. All of the seats and podiums were engraved with fanciful depictions of pocket dragons and men.

This looks more like a cathedral than a courtroom, he thought, peering around. Not only was it beautiful, but the place seemed also equipped to properly accommodate both dragons and humans. Lining the observer and jury wall like a balcony in a theatre were rows of tiny, pocket dragon sized seats that could have occupied hundreds of dragons— which today were nearly packed with viewers. Similar seats awaited them at one of the desks in front of the judge's podium.

"The Dragon Courthouse," Azara mused beside him, as if reading his thoughts. "This place was designed specifically for dealings between pocket dragons and human kind. Likewise, the rules here are going to be different from that of an ordinary court, but it's still mostly human terms."

They alighted down on a table to the right of the judge's stand. It was only now that the prickling sensation of eyes on him set in. He scanned around, looking at the various people gathered in the back to observe and those from the jury. Who they were and why they were there he didn't know, though there was no one that he recognized. Some had tanned skin, as if originating from somewhere very hot, whereas others looked more suited to colder weather.

His attention then turned to the judge. He was not the gaunt, grim, well-kept human that Angus had been imagining— quite the opposite. In fact, it was not a *he* at all. The woman in the judge's podium
looked *young* even, with delicate features,

somewhat frazzled black hair that she was currently busy tucking behind her ear, and...

Her feet on the desk?

Oh no, Angus thought. *Oh no oh no oh no oh no,* he realized.

Clara.

He whipped towards Azara and spoke in a wild hushed whisper. "Clara is here! Clara is here! She's the judge! We're all doomed! I told you this wouldn't end well! Now she can cheat and we'll lose and pocket dragon kind is doomed and how in the great fluffy sheep did Clara become the judge?"

Azara's face was contorted with thought, yet it was Eoghan on his other side that answered him. "The same way we would have with any other judge," he answered calmly.

Angus's ears went as flat as the expression on his face. "I'm sorry, but I don't think you understand the situation," he pointed a talon at Clara. "She is insane. I know several *sheep* who I would rather have as a judge, and most of *them* at least don't go around trying to kill you with ice cream!" He insisted. "There has got to be—"

Bang! Bang! Bang!

Clara slammed her gavel down onto her table, calling for the trial to begin. She didn't bother to correct her posture as a grave silence settled in the courtroom. "Bring in the defendant!" She summoned, gesturing with a lazy wave of her gavel.

Beside him, Eoghan frowned. "She doesn't know anything about being a judge, does she?" He whispered. "Because it sounds like her concept of it is either few hundred years outmoded or learned from a really bad murder mystery film."

Before Angus could say anything in response, the door on the left opened and in walked...

"Mr. S!" Angus whispered under his breath. *Oh no... Oh my sheep...* his gaze darted between the expressionless man and the bored-looking woman. *This was planned. We are definitely, absolutely doomed.*

Then Angus's eyes traveled to the strange, white mop atop Mr. S's head... "WHY is Mr. S wearing a SHEEP on his head?" Angus whispered to Azara.

"It's not a sheep," Azara replied. "It's a... wig thing. Some strange human tradition that the lawyers wear them," she muttered.

"Hmph," Angus murmured, glaring at the sheep-wig-thing.

And Mr. S wasn't alone, accompanied by a broad, general-like man who Angus didn't recognize. To the right of Azara, however, he noticed Frida flinch at the sight of him and Isis's eyes narrowed. Clearly Isis and Frida had encountered this man before.

Bang!

Their attention was snapped back up towards Clara with another slam of her gavel. The edge of her lip was curved in the slightest of grins that made ice race down Angus's spine.

"Let the trial begin!" She announced. Mr. S and the gruff man took a seat— and Angus caught the former shoot Clara a firm glare from underneath his shades that could mean little else but *get your shoes off the table!* Yet Clara seemed perfectly content to remain as she was.

"Dragons, present your case," she ordered, looking thoroughly bored yet at the same time making her voice sound commanding.

Angus didn't realize he was supposed to say anything until he received a gentle shove in the back from Azara's wing. He stumbled forward till he reached the edge of the table closest to the judge's podium. He tried to summon up words, yet before he could voice any of them, Eoghan was at his side and speaking.

"Your Honor," the green dragon began, adjusting his glasses on his narrow snout. His voice was slow and very much lawyer-like. "We are here on the matter of the dragon kidnapping. For the past three weeks— yet possibly quite longer than that— dragons have been captured and taken to a facility where they were held against their will. Some reports even extend to experimentation and—"

"Yeah yeah," the judge interrupted, picking at her fingernails. "We get it. Now get to the point."

Eoghan looked exasperated but gave him a look that clearly meant *your turn,* and so Angus summoned up his courage once more and spoke. "We and many other dragons were captured. After an awful inspecting process, Azara and I were sold as pets. We were the pets of a boy in Willough until two people, a man and a woman, from the lab came and started chasing us through the woods, shooting at us. Then—"

"That's quite enough," Clara interrupted. "I don't have all day so speed it up or we're going right to the defendant."

Yet before Angus could even open his mouth, Clara interrupted him again. "Nothing to add? Great! Let's get on with it," she said. She swung her gavel around to indicate to Mr. S and the gruff man. "Defendant, state your case."

"With pleasure," Mr. S said, rising from his seat and adjusting his suit as he did. "I would firstly like to indicate that there is no proof to the existence of this 'lab'. There is further no proof as to the existence of any illegal dragon pet store anywhere in London from which these dragons could have been sold. Furthermore, there is no way to prove this ‘chase through the woods’ as you call it in which you were supposedly shot at actually happened; and for all of these instances, there are no credible human witnesses. Therefore, these dragon's claims are invalid," he concluded.

Clara slowly nodded her head, making a convincing considering-judge act. "You prove a good point, Mr. S. You have a valid point in that there were no *credible human* witnesses. I believe this is enough to draw on to conclude that—"

"Objection!" Eoghan shouted. "You must allow us to present our evidence," he insisted.

"Hmmm..." Clara mused. "Very well, present your 'evidence'," she said, then suddenly cracked her gavel down on the desk. "But if you ever interrupt me again, dragon, I'll have you thrown in jail," she warned.

Angus, his fear starting to dissipate under his anger at the injustice, said: "Our first piece of evidence is the car. During the chase, the man and woman's car drove into a stream. It was black, from my memory. You can also observe countless bullet holes marking the trees nearby, sure evidence of the chase," he stated, his confidence growing. He tried not to be unnerved by Mr. S's expressionless stare as the man watched him, or distracted by his constant tapping on his strange black watch. "... And then there is the dragon shop, which can also be investigated. There, hundreds of dragons are being kept and sold under the radar. This shop is connected to the lab, where thousands more dragons are held."

Before Clara or Mr. S could cut them off, Eoghan jumped in. "May I suggest a recess for some teams to be dispatched to the aforementioned locations to confirm this evidence? The woods of Willough are close enough that I believe a two hour recess would be adequate time."

Clara made a show of looking as if she was considering it, and said: "Very well, I'll have two teams sent out."

Something's not right... Angus thought, narrowing his eyes. *Why would she agree to it this easily... If she knew it would prove us right?*

Clara then continued. "We could go to recess, I suppose...."

"Or, Your Honor, if I may suggest something else to fill the time while the teams are out inspecting their evidence," Mr. S intervened.

The judge raised her eyebrows as if surprised. "Yes, Mr. S? What do you suggest?"

An uneasy feeling settled in Angus's stomach as he observed this conversation that sounded all too pre-planned...

Mr. S pulled out a shiny black briefcase from underneath the desk and laid it out on the table. "While we are all gathered here, I thought there was another issue that we might as well address while we are on the subject of the rights of dragons."

"And what might that be, Mr. S?" The judge replied, sounding just a bit bored, as if her words had been rehearsed.

Mr. S laid his hands atop his briefcase. "I think it's about time we settled the matter of dragons, once and for all," he announced.

The unease in Angus's belly solidified into a dead weight at these words. *How did they do this?* He thought in a hopeless daze. *They were planning to turn this trial around from the start...* He realized. *This was all a trap... A way to beat us at our own game, kill two dragons with one stone... Because if they can affect dragon rights before the evidence teams get back...*

Then the evidence won't matter at all.

Clara made a good show of looking fascinated. "An intriguing concept! We might as well, as we are all here on a trial regarding such matters already..." She grinned, and slammed her gavel down on her desk once more. "It shall be so! Let us discuss the matter of dragons while we wait for the teams to return."

"Object— " Eoghan began to protest.

"That's enough!" Clara interrupted fiercely, swinging her legs down to the floor. "I told you that if I had one more peep from you I would throw you out of this court." She fondled her mallet as if contemplating how easily it could squish a dragon. There was then a ding from what Angus presumed her black watch, identical to S's. She glanced down at it and mused. "But... I'll be generous. You may remain here for... Legal reasons. But you will not be allowed to speak." Eoghan looked ready to object, but the judge cut him off yet again. "Tsk tsk! Should you happen to make a single squeak," The look in her gaze blatantly indicated that she wanted to add 'like the rat you are' to her sentence, "I'll make sure you never speak again."

Anger and fear flared within Angus. *Never speak again...* Her words echoed in his mind. *Those dragons in Willough...* He considered. *What was that William had said? The dragons of Willough haven't spoken in years... That was it.* Angus narrowed his eyes. *There must be a connection...*

Before he could hypothesize any further, Clara continued: "Very well then, Mr. S, where do you wish to begin?"

Mr. S popped open his briefcase, which appeared to be filled with papers. "I believe an analysis of all the many matters in which dragons have damaged our world would be suitable," he said. "And I believe it would make sense to start with the crime committed by dragons against human kind."

The judge nodded. "Brilliant idea. Please begin," she said decidedly.

Angus glanced around at the other dragons on the desk with him. Azara looked like she was ready to disembowel the judge. Isis's eyes were narrowed, calculating, thinking. Eoghan looked miffed and frustrated. Frida looked like she wanted to sink through the floor and disappear.

Angus at first felt quite like the little ice dragon at the moment. *The trial has been flipped... Now we are the defendants... Fighting for all of dragon kind...* Then he thought of Azara, her anger... *This isn't right. The way they speak to us, the way they try to degrade us... It must change.* Then he thought of Isis. *Now we just need to be smart enough and clever enough to bring justice and equality to our world.*

So he turned to look at Mr. S. *Come on you sheep-headed robot,* he thought determinedly. *Throw us all your wooly nonsense.*

"Thank you, Your Honor," Mr. S began, pawing through his briefcase and grabbing various neat packets of papers. "I will begin with numbers, as those are undeniable facts, and math is the basis of the human world." He held in front of him a packet of papers, though it was too far away for Angus to read what was written on it. "Firstly, twenty percent of crime in the world is committed by dragons." He paused a moment, letting it sink in. "Let me emphasize twenty percent. Imagine how many lives would have been saved, how many injuries prevented, how many people not robbed from, if dragons hadn't been granted the privilege of rights among us, protecting them, when we really should be looking out for our own."

Clara slowly nodded her head. "You prove a good point. Please go on."

"With pleasure," Mr. S said, quickly flipping through his packet as he resumed. "Dragons also damage our economy. With their skill in thievery they steal from us, with their powers they harm us; causing expensive costs both medical and mental. They damage our businesses, our houses, our cities. They infest all of those and dirty our streets like vermin. It is quite like us giving a rat a right to spread disease— our giving dragons rights."

"That is true, Mr. S," The judge responded unenthusiastically. She lazily inspected the gavel, not bothering even to look at them as she said: "Dragons, give your defense. If you have any."

Angus wanted to roar at how wrong, how biased it all was. At how humans commit such far worse crimes to the dragons without care or thought and get away with it almost every time. *But no,* he told himself firmly. *This must be done just right.*

It's just a matter of how.

And at that moment, the observer area's door swung open.

Baaaaaaaaaaaaaaa!

And through the doors stepped an elderly Irish man, carrying none other than a lamb in his arms.

"What is this nonsense! Bloody *nonsense!*" The Irishman bellowed as he hobbled down the center aisle towards the judge's podium. He was wearing an odd combination of tan working pants and a simple white yet slightly dirty shirt with a silver suit jacket and matching hat.

Clara banged her gavel down a couple times. "Sir, please silence yourself and remove the sheep. There will be no sheep in the courtroom," she ordered.

Yet the man continued on unabated. He seemed... Familiar, somehow. He was old with short silver hair and muttonchops, looking like a bizarre combination of farm worker and businessman. "Remove the sheep? No *sir!* Absolutely not!" He denied, hefting the lamb in his arms and sauntering right up to the desk where Angus and the other dragons sat. "Harvey here's taken ill, I flew all the way from Ireland with him to make sure he's cared for on my trip. The sheep stays."

Baaaaaaaaaa! The lamb agreed.

Clara sighed. "Very well sir, just make sure he stays contained and behaved,"

"Aha! See there," The man said ecstatically. "That is the problem. Why is it that you will make allowances, change the rules, for an animal that could care less either way? And why then, do you stand so adamant in making sure the dragons have about as much rights as Harvey here?" He pointed out.

"Sir, who are you? You must halt this interruption or we will have you thrown out of the courtroom!" Clara warned.

The man bowed, sheep and all, taking off his hat. "I am Mr. Alastair Alby, Director of Tourism at the Giant's Causeway. And as soon as I heard news of a dragon matching the description of my helpful little friend being in a trial down in London, I came right away," he explained.

That explains the disheveled clothes... And why he was so familiar! Angus realized. He had gotten glimpses of the man in his office now and again, though he'd never spoken to him.

Clara looked like she desperately wanted to roll her eyes, but instead said: "Well then Mr. Alby, is there something you wish to say in these dragon's defense, or are you simply here to waste our time?"

Alastair fitted his hat back atop his head, his face a clear picture of shock. "Why of course I have something to say! I heard most of it — those shady men standing outside wouldn't let me in for the longest time. But I heard the gist of it and I *say* Your Honor: Rubbish!"

Baaaaa Baaaaaaaaa! Harvey emphasized.

"I say Your Honor," Mr. Alby continued, and he pointed down straight at Angus with a rough finger. "This dragon has increased tourism at the Giant's Causeway *tenfold*! And *I'm* the Director— I know my numbers! Already it was a popular place, but the tourists that came to see the dragon from the story alone was nearly half my business! They would see him lurking round, see a tail or talon or a glimpse of an eye hiding in the hills and stones and they loved it! The advertisement I could do with it-— *"Come see the Giant's Causeway— And catch a glimpse of the Dragon of the Legend!"* It brought in thousands more tourists!" The man fumbled to hold his lamb with one hand and dig through a back pocket with another. He produced his wallet, which he them fished through with one hand, spilling assorted cards onto the courtroom floor in the process. Finally, he held up a card and let his wallet fall to the ground. "Look here! A little snapshot that some tourist got— it made them all go wild to come!" He held out the wallet photo for all to see, showing it to the judge and Mr. S and the observers and jury and finally the dragons.

Angus's face contorted into mortification.

There, on the photograph, was his tail. His tail curled around a pillar of hexagonal stones. Angus glanced down at his tail currently curled over his talons and blinked. *My tail brought thousands of tourists to the Giant's Causeway,* he thought. *Great.*

Mr. Alby set down Harvey on the dragon's desk next to Angus as he bent down to pick up his wallet and cards. The lamb instantly laid down, and Angus absentmindedly stroked its fluffy head with his talon as the man continued. "So if you are here saying that dragons are bad for business, I say rubbish! What they do that helps us far exceeds what they do that harms us," he said firmly. "I've got a friend in the army who got shot through the lung last year. Said he would be dead for sure! But no— there was a dragon at the hospital who healed him! Now he's livin' an' breath'n' just fine!" He argued. "And you say that dragons steal from us— and that I'm sure some do— but others help us! Knew a guy who runs a jewelry shop in Ireland— it once got robbed blind. But a dragon hid in the thief's pocket, found his stash, and led the police right to him! Ha!"

Clara looked absolutely flabbergasted. Mr. S was furiously tapping on his watch, looking quite paler than usual. Yet Clara seemed oblivious to the persistent dings on her own watch. "I... See, sir. We will have your information confirmed... But for now... Mr. S?

Do you have any other points you wish to discuss?"

Mr. S gave her a flat look, which was perhaps the closest thing to emotion Angus had ever seen on the agent's face. It almost looked comical beneath his sheep wig. But nevertheless, he said: "Yes, I do." He clicked shut his briefcase.

"Very good," Clara said, her confidence growing again. "Mr. Alby, if you would please take a seat. For now, until we can check your numbers and facts, we shall consider your uninvited speech inadmissible."

Mr. Alby looked furious. "Inadmissible? Why *sir—* "

"Mr. Alby, if you cannot keep quiet, then we will have to have you removed from the courtroom," Clara snapped. The man continued to look furious, but he kept his mouth closed and pulled up a seat next to the dragon's table, stroking his lamb. "Thank you, Mr. Alby," Clara said, her voice dripping with sarcasm. "Now, please continue, Mr. S."

"Thank you, Clara," Mr. S acted, straightening his watch on his wrist and restoring himself to his full posture as he announced:

"I would like to discuss the effects dragons have had upon humanity since the very beginning."

22

Dragons of the Ages

Frida watched the trial play out in horror.

She had been meant to explain the situation in The Glass Cage, their experience inside the lab. Yet now... Now that was all out the window until the teams returned.

She cast her glance to a clock ticking away on the wall behind them. Half an hour had expired since they had supposedly left— an hour and a half until they returned.

An hour and a half to make sure the judge didn't completely obliterate their rights. The judge— their insane, anti-dragon judge. Frida had overheard Angus call her Clara. *Such a pretty name,* Frida mused, *for such a nasty person.*

Now Frida just shifted on her talons, keeping her head low, wishing that she could be anywhere, anywhere but here right now. *Of all dragons... I really shouldn't be one of the dragons that all of pocket dragon kind is relying upon to keep their rights... I don't even know what to say...* "Please continue, Mr. S," Clara requested.

Frida turned her head to the silly yet blank faced looking man on what had previously been the defendant's side, and listened as he spoke. "Dragons have been affecting and corrupting our society for as long as we have been around," he began. "They have posed as false deities," he said, pointing a finger at Isis. The golden dragon looked like she was trying very hard to keep her mouth closed.

"They have lead us around, imposing themselves upon our cultures. Who knows what we might have been if they had not been allowed to affect us," he lectured. "Perhaps we wouldn't have had any world wars. Perhaps we would have cured cancer years earlier than we did if dragons hadn't kept multiple civilizations in barbarity. Perhaps we would have set up our space stations faster if we hadn't been distracted by their magic."

Frida felt her spark light within her at these accusations. Yet it quickly extinguished in fear again, as she knew no way she could help counter such a question— for who could know what the world would be like if dragons had been hunted and eliminated, if they had been vanquished from human society? *Perhaps it would have been better...* Frida considered. *Yet...*

It equally could have also been worse.

"Furthermore," Mr. S continued. "They have infiltrated our lives. They have made themselves a part of our religions and cultures, affecting us in who knows how many ways today. Long ago the dragons wormed their way into Aztec culture, having them perform rituals involving plants for no logical reason. Who knows what sort of culture the Aztecs might have become if the dragons hadn't inserted themselves!" The barrister explained, somehow managing to sneer with a completely emotionless face. "And today— there are villages around the world that are dependent on dragons! They weasel their way into these families and homes for free food and shelter and make sure the humans rely upon their magic to survive, forever trapping them in a vicious cycle."

"And so," he concluded. "We must do something now before they can corrupt us any further."

The judge nodded her head. "I completely agre—"

"I have something to say!" Frida burst. Fear blossomed through her body, cold as ice, as all eyes turned on her. She resisted the urge to shrink away from them, and added: "In... Our defense."

Clara narrowed her eyes. "DON'T interrupt the judge, *dragon,*" she growled. "But... You may speak," she mused.

Frida felt as if she had turned to ice, but somehow she managed to shuffle out to the edge of the desk. "I... I come from one of those villages that Mr. S speaks of. It is not as he says it is," she started meekly.

Clara frowned. "What was that? Speak up, little dragon. If we can't hear you... We'll just have to skip you."

Frida glared back up at the wild-haired-woman, and took a breath. "I said I come from one of the villages that Mr. S speaks of!" She said more loudly. "It is not as he says it is. We are in coexistence. Yes... They give me food. And in return, I help them. I haven't forced them into anything. I was saved before I had hatched. All I do is help..."

Clara knitted her brows together and leaned forward. "And do you have any evidence of this?" She said in a mockingly sweet voice.

"I.. Eh..." Frida struggled with Clara's question. *If they won't listen to me anyway, what good would it do?* She thought despairingly. *How could they possibly believe me if I said "a remote village in Siberia?"*

Clara leaned back in her seat, grinning. "I thought so."

Frida felt crushed. "It— it's in Siberia..." She tried weakly.

Clara only retained her smirk. "That's hardly proof."

"I... I tended their fires! I made sure they all didn't freeze in the cold..." She tried.

Clara raised an eyebrow. "And then you intended to burn them all I presume? Fascinating! I believe we shall have to do some further inquiry on you..."

Frida's heart dropped. "No— no not at all—"

"There will be nothing of the sort!" Called a man from the observer seating. They all whipped around to see an old man bolt to his feet. He had a wrinkled, kind face, stormy blue eyes...

"Kostya!" Frida felt the corners of her eyes well with tears. *Kostya is here! He found me!*

Kostya strode down the aisle and took up a position where the Irishman had previously stood. "I am Kostya Kliment, and I am from the village of which Frida speaks. I am the one who rescued her as an egg," he announced, staring fiercely up at the judge. He then turned his head, the corners of his eyes crinkling as his face instantly softened, looking down at her. "Frida..." He said, his voice so mournful yet joyous. He reached out a hand to her, inviting her. "I knew it was you when you said Siberia..."

Frida smiled, and jumped into the air. She glided up and landed on his shoulder. She felt that if she spoke, her words would wobble, and so she simply smiled, overjoyed.

"I've been looking for you ever since the day you disappeared," he said, lifting a finger and gently stroking her little cheek.

Clara scowled, looking annoyed out of her mind. "Can we *please* stop with these uninvited interruptions!?" She complained, flinging her arms out in emphasis. She let them fall with a sigh, then tucked a stray piece of hair behind her ear. "Well then, *sir*, what is it you wish to say?"

Kostya turned his stern-sailor gaze back to the judge. "I wish to lay confirmation to this dragon's words. What she says is true: There is a village in the far reaches of Siberia where I and several others live. Frida maintains her fires for us so that we can live there and never freeze. I've raised her since her hatching, and she has no reason to ever try any of the wretched things you accuse her of. She is loved by the village but not worshipped. And her magic allows us to do something incapable by humans alone— live a simple life, a life we want, in the coldest depths of Russia. Without Frida, we would not be able to live this way— the way we want to live. Free of most machinery and distraction," he said. "So you see, dragons *are* good for our society."

Clara was running a finger along her mallet out of boredom. "Your statements are both flawed and inadmissible." She sounded as if she was getting very tired of this trial. "I presume, living without most machinery, that you have no... phone... Or photographs... Or anything else with which to prove your little fairyland exists? Or more to the point, that you are telling the truth about anything at all?"

Kostya opened and closed his mouth like a codfish in outrage, yet before he could speak, the doors on the left side of the room swung open.

"That will not be necessary," Said a broad-shouldered man in a suit and shades—

Lab attire, Frida recalled. *This can't be good.*

"We have returned from Willough and the shop that the dragon's talked about. We have returned with photographs of their 'evidence'," he announced, swinging a satchel off his shoulder and onto the previously defendant desk. He pawed through it until he produced a stack of laminated photographs; the man then picked up the first three, and rotated around to display them to all.

He finally faced them, and Frida's heart sank.

"As you can see," the man said. "There is no car, no dragon shop," he paused for emphasis.

"And no lab."

23
The Great Pocket Dragon Trial

Anger surged through Azara, so fierce that she had left little pinprick holes in the wood of the desk from digging her talons in—so that she wouldn't launch herself into Clara's face and show the wild-haired-woman what a *real* bad hair day looked like.

She stared at the photographs in disbelief, wanting to tear them to shreds. *They've cleaned up their evidence. How did they do that so quickly? It's impossible!* Yet they somehow had-— the first photograph showed the creek with no sign of the black vehicle or the blue truck. The next showed what had previously been the dragon store— but instead of a shop full of cages of dragons, there was just a vacant, empty storefront. Even the glass had been repaired; not a trace remained of the secret black market shop nor of the dramatic escape that the other dragons had made from it.

The third photograph was taken from the inside of the empty building. Where there had been rows of miniature cages there was only flat, wallpapered wall. Even the cashier desk had been removed. And behind it, where there had been a door leading into the lab...

There was only a wall.

She got a little brush on her wing from Angus beside her, who glanced down. She followed his gaze down to where the wood had been shredded beneath her talons. She instantly retracted them, but her stern glare quickly returned to the lab man, full of anger. *There has to be something I can do...*

After displaying the rest of his pictures, all showing similar frustratingly cleaned-up scenes, he returned the photographs to his satchel. "So you see, these dragon's claims are false," he said before pulling up a seat next to Mr. S and Mr. K.

Clara nodded her head consideringly. "Your evidence is quite convincing...." Her fingers closed around the handle of her gavel, and she wavered it around in the air...

Bang!

It slammed down, the echo sounding like a death knell to Azara. "Based on these findings," Clara announced. "I declare the defendants of the lab trial, not guilty! And furthermore, the case and accusations against any such 'lab', are hereby closed, seeing as none of the events mentioned had actually happened and all of the locations were imaginary."

No... It can't be... Azara felt as if the world was slowing down around her. *No...*

The man who had been referred to as Mr. K then stood. "While this has now been resolved, I do believe that the matter of the dragon's rights has not yet been concluded...? I would like to say something on this," he said.

The judge was twirling her gavel between her fingers. "Yes, Keeper-Mr. K," She corrected herself, looking ever so slightly paler at her slip. She swung her legs back up onto the judge's podium and crossed them. "Please proceed," she said, continuing to fiddle with the gavel.

Mr. K straightened his suit and strode around the table towards the podium. By now, the man Kostya had seated himself on the dragon's side, looked flabbergasted, leaving the floor open for the dark-suited man. "Let me point out, that dragons are as insignificant as mice. The only difference between them," he grinned. "Is that they're shiny and are good at parlor tricks." He lazily strode about the courtroom floor with his hands in his pockets as he talked, his words slow for emphasis. "We let ourselves be influenced, be controlled by these little rats. We let them destroy our cultures, damage our economy, affect our world! Why... I ask you... Do we let this happen?" He paused right in front of the judge's podium. "Why... I ask... Do we let ourselves be led by *mice*?"

Clara rested her elbow on the podium and then her chin in her palm. "Might you have a... Solution for this quandary, Mr. K?"

If it was possible for Azara's heart to fall any further, it did. *This sounds wrong... They aren't just seeking to defend themselves...*

But to completely destroy us.

"Indeed I do, Your Honor," Mr. K confirmed. "I have been working with an organization that has been developing a solution to our little dragon problem," he began. "Our solution... Is called The Habitat."

The little ice dragon Frida gasped, and Isis's ears had flattened. The latter whispered, possibly to herself but Azara still heard it: "The Habitat... That is what they called our cage."

Understanding swept through her. *They weren't only trying to bring us down... They are going to try and get their horrific plan... What they did to all those poor dragons... Legalized!*

The broad-shouldered, hulk of a man continued. "Our Dragon Rehabilitation And Care Objective, or DRACO, will humanely remove dragons from our world. With underground facilities located all over the world, we have artificial environments we call Habitats, that can house between five-thousand and ten-thousand dragons comfortably. With multiple Habitat's per facility, we can relocate all of the worlds' dragons beneath the surface, where they will cease to interfere with our lives. We will also help by preserving this delicate species." The edge of his lip curled up. "Safe, underground, out of our way, forever."

His words rang in her ears.

Underground...

Out of the way...

Forever.

She could hear the fearful hushed whispering from the observing dragons on their little balcony. These words were clearly echoing in their minds as well— the prospect of being locked away underground... Some dragons were gliding out the windows, as if they could fly so hard and so fast as to escape the peril brewing inside this cauldron courtroom.

"The DRACO plan seems like a perfect solution to our problem!" Clara declared. She raised her gavel again. "I hereby declare—!"

"OBJECTION!" Azara roared, her voice echoing throughout the room.

Clara froze, her gavel still in the air. She cocked it like a crow as she slowly lowered her arm. "Yes?"

Azara spread her wings and pushed off the desk. She flapped up till she was directly before the judge's podium, and hovered there, meeting Clara's wild brown eyes with her own silver ones. "I have a way to prove that there is a lab, and that this DRACO plan is not... Humane," she growled, carefully choosing a term that she could fight with.

Clara narrowed her eyes, looking like a bird inspecting a delicious worm. "Very well... Try," she dared.

Azara rotated around to face the rest of the courtroom. She took a steadying breath, closing her eyes... *It's the only way...* She told herself, and snapped open her eyes. "I can prove this... Because I am a telempath," she announced.

"A what?" The judge laughed.

Azara whirled around to face her again. "A telempath! A combination of telepath and empath. But that doesn't matter— what does is that I can tell when someone is telling the truth..." She grinned just a slight as her confidence grew. "Or is lying."

Clara still looked skeptical. "*Really?* There's no way to prove it." She began to raise her mallet again—

Azara swooped down and hovered before the jury. "Everyone, make a line!" She ordered. "I'll prove it— ask me a question, and I'll tell if it's a truth or a lie," she called out. A couple of people slowly rose from their seats, curious. "Come on, everyone!" She beckoned. "Let me show you that I tell the truth!"

Gradually, her heart rose as all of the jury members lifted from their seats and began to form a line before her. Azara smiled as she flew down to the eye level of the first person in the line.

The woman before her wore a simple black suit, though not like those of the lab. "Ask your question," Azara prompted.

The woman looked thoughtful for a moment, then said: "My favorite color is black."

Azara focused on the woman as she said this... On the mental waves that emanated from her... "That's a lie," she answered,

The woman looked surprised— and impressed, and nodded. "It's actually white."

Clara was less impressed. "Fifty fifty chance! She just as easily could have been wrong! Besides, that was an easy one!"

Azara turned back to the line again and motioned for the next person to come up: this time, a young man with brown hair and matching eyes. "My favorite books are 'the Infinity series,'" he said.

Azara focused just as she had before... "Truth," she finally said.

The young man nodded. "Yes!"

Clara said nothing, but she was leaning back in her chair, scowling with her arms crossed. Mr. S's face was grim, and Mr. K was turning red.

The questions continued... Favorite animal... Birth date... Employment... On and on, until she reached the last person, who was asking if her favorite breakfast food was a pamplemousse.

"Truth!" Azara answered.

"Correct!" The happy woman laughed.

As the last observer returned to her seat, Azara turned to face the judge once more. "So, Your Honor, if I may, I would like to question Mr. K." Without waiting for an answer, she zipped down so that she was face to face with the red-faced broad man in the center front of the courtroom. "Tell me, Mr. K, is the DRACO plan humane?"

His angry eyes fixed her in a hard stare. "Yes, it is."

Azara listened to the mental vibrations... As she expected, they reverberated negatively within her. "That's a lie," she announced.

There was a stirring in the jury as they began to whisper among themselves.

Before she could be interrupted, Azara was quick with another question. "Does the lab exist?"

The man turned as red as a beet. "No!" He growled.

Azara grinned as the vibrations told her otherwise. "Another lie!"

The noise amidst the observers grew louder. Above, Azara could hear the excited rustling of wings and talons.

"Is everything that Frida, Angus and Isis said true? Is the lab kidnapping dragons? Is the lab selling dragons, and cruelly trapping others?" She persisted.

"No. No. No!" He snarled slowly, looking like it was taking everything he had to keep his calm.

Azara felt the mental waves so thick and she could have ridden them. She cocked her head, paying attention to each one very, very carefully...

"Lie, lie, lie."

Azara could feel the tension in the air at her words. She turned away from the red-faced man and looked towards the jury— the people who now turned over in their minds what they had seen, what they had heard, and in whose favor they were.

They were deciding. They had seen her magic at work— seen that she told the truth of her powers, each individual trying her, accepting for themselves what she could do. From the man who liked the Infinity series to the woman who liked pamplemousses for breakfast, Azara studied the subtle expressions on their faces... As they decided whose side they were on. Who they believed. Even the sheep seemed contemplative.

“I think it’s time we consult the jury,” Clara said slowly, studying the faces of the people. “I’m sure they don’t need any more time to decide." She finally turned to the jury. "Jury, have you reached a decision?"

Azara watched them as they whispered amongst themselves. She counted her heartbeats.

One.

Two.

Three.

It felt like a million had passed when the forewoman stood. It was the same woman whose favourite colour was white. "We have, your Honor."

Clara nodded and growled, "Then read it already."

The forewoman fingered the tiny slip of white paper in her hand. "We the jury, find the pocket dragons, not guilty."

Azara almost didn't believe it.

Clearly Clara felt the same.

The judge stared at the jury, her expression dumbfounded. She had heard it—heard that if she decreed against the dragons...

The jury and observers would see the corruption, see the blatant lies... See the entire setup; See that it wasn't right.

Disbelief clear over her face, Clara raised her gavel...

And slammed it down.

"The verdict is in favor of... the pocket dragons."

24
Sunset

Waves of orange and pink stained the horizon at dusk, the sun sending golden ripples across the sky and casting the low hanging clouds in a shadow of purple. Long shadows danced among the city below as people continued their celebration in the streets.

Isis sat on the rim of the amber peak of the Dragon Courthouse, a gentle smile playing on her lips as she watched the joyous festivities below. Cool winds teased her wings, inviting her to ride them to warmer drafts.

Yet for now... She was content to rest, to enjoy this victory.

A green and golden mess of scales and wing membrane half-tumbled-half-flew haphazardly towards the rim. "HEY Mr. Teleman..." He sang as he flew, collapsing on his back into the rim beside her. "Telempath BANANA!" He bellowed. The Irish dragon happily scrabbled to his talons. "Seven foot eight talon nine talon BUNCH!" He flung out his talons excitedly, falling once more backwards...

When Azara swooped in and caught his back, propping him back into his talons before setting down beside him. "You," Azara joked, grinning. "Have spent far too much time dancing."

She felt an icy but gentle presence on her other side as Frida set down besides Isis.

Meanwhile, Angus continued to ramble. "But it was so FUN!" He protested. "The entire courtroom— a conga line! And that guy with his face as red as a tomato angrily spinning around in circles— he was like the centerpiece of a carousel!" The green dragon insisted. He then flung out his wings and talons again. "Daylight come and me want to go hoOME!" He sang.

Azara chuckled, steadying him from falling over again with a talon. "Easy there mate."

Isis smiled and gave a contented sigh. "I didn't know how we were going to get through that. But we did," she murmured, letting her eyes meet each of the gathered dragons. "We survived, we brought an end to the lab, we beat them at their own twisted game."

It was now Azara's turn to tumble towards Angus, causing the Irish dragon to collide into Isis and Isis to be squished into Frida, making a sandwich of sorts. "Well done all!" Azara announced happily. The blue dragon's gaze suddenly turned thoughtful. "Hey, Angus, did you ever find out what happened to William?"

Angus scrunched up his face. "Yeah... We sort of left him on the pavement after being knocked out cold by ice cream..." He chuckled. "No pun intended."

"Hm," Azara shrugged. "I hope he'll be alright. He was a nice kid."

Angus nodded. "That he was," he answered. "But I'm sure he's fine. Probably hitchhiked some busses back to Willough by now. All safe and cozy— hey, maybe he'll even use what he's learned to free the other dragons of Willough. Let it be the dragon's choice whether or not to stay."

Azara smiled. "That's a nice thought." Her gaze then turned distant. "I noticed something strange about what Clara said during the trial... About making sure we never speak again..." She bit her lip. "I think maybe... Maybe the lab did that to the dragons. To keep them... Quiet."

Isis nodded in agreement. "I'll talk to the queen about that. We'll see what we can do—

maybe we can return the dragon's voices to them."

Angus grinned. "The dragons of Willough shall speak again."

Isis glanced again towards the setting sun. She had gone weeks without seeing a sunset... And somehow that made this one all the more beautiful. A thought occurred to her, and she turned her head towards Angus and Azara to her right. "Where are you going to be going after this?" She asked. "Back to your homes?"

Angus and Azara exchanged grins, and Azara finally said: "I think I've had enough of London for now... Need a little break," she explained. "Angus was going to show me Ireland— take me to the Giant's Causeway, try riding some sheep. I need a bit of a soft and fluffy getaway."

Isis smiled. "Have fun on your ventures," she bid. "You deserve a good vacation." She then turned to face the gentle presence to her left, dual colored eyes peering at her thoughtfully. "And you Frida, where do you think you will go?" A hope flickered within her that perhaps the shy little dragon might wish to come with her. For after all of their trials, she had grown fond of her.

"I'm going back to Siberia," Frida answered. "Back to my village with Kostya. The frost dragons from The Glass Cage have decided to join me, so I'm going to help them set up there-— most of their original homes are too hard to get back to," she explained. A smile tugged at the frost dragon's lips. "And Kostya... He has a story he wants to show me."

Isis saddened a bit, but smiled nonetheless. "It was a pleasure, Frida. And you are always welcome in Egypt, should you ever feel like a change in temperature."

Frida beamed. "Thank you, Isis." She then turned to look at a sparkly figure in the distance, flying towards them. It soon became apparent that this figure was a dragon...

"My queen!" Isis welcomed with a bow, the other dragons around her following suit as the Dragon Queen came and landed next to Frida.

The elegant dragon shook her head and smiled. "I'll never get used to that. Please, rise," she encouraged. She looked... different from when Isis had seen her in The Glass Cage and after their escape. She had clearly cleaned her scales, for they shined pure and pristine against the last of the light. She also now had a crown around her horns – Simple yet beautiful, with silver lacing metal studded with sapphires. Besides that, however, she was only adorned with a simple silver necklace with an azurite pocket dragon emblem.

"Sorry, Your Majesty," Isis apologized with a rueful smile. "It's habit."

"Do not worry," answered the queen. She then turned towards Frida. "Frida, I am so glad that I have finally a chance to speak with you. I had wanted to as soon as we escaped... But things got busy."

The meek frost dragon shifted on her talons. "You... Wanted to speak with me?" Frida said, sounding somewhere between curious and terrified.

The queen nodded. "Yes," she answered. "Frida, were you born in Siberia?"

The icy dragon's dual colored eyes widened. "...Yes," she confirmed.

The queen pressed tentatively on. "Do you know of a dragon named Embla?"

Frida looked confused and shook her head. "... No...?"

The queen looked vaguely disappointed, and thought for a moment before asking: "Your parents— did they have your same magick?"

Frida's face turned distant. "I... I don't know. I never knew them. My adoptive father, Kostya, he found me as an egg in the middle of the woods some years ago..."

The queen suddenly became attentive again. "A few years ago? Perhaps, ten years ago?"

Frida was starting to look alarmed, and Isis cocked her head in confusion. "Yes... Why?" The former answered meekly.

A cascade of emotions flew across the queen's face, from surprise to joy to thrill. Suddenly the queen took a step back, tilted her snout down and breathed a fire to life into her talon. The fire then proceeded to dance and thrive in the queen's talon without any nourishment... and it radiated *cold.* "Frida," The queen said slowly. "My sister disappeared in Siberia, ten years ago."

Frida looked shocked, then she stuttered: "That— does that… Are you saying?"

The queen smiled. "Frida, I believe you are my niece." She announced. The royal dragon let the fire in her talon spin and twist and alter its color. "The gift of this sort of magic, it's one only my family has been known to have. When I saw you use it back at the lab— I had a feeling. That... And you look exactly like my sister," she explained. "So I suppose that would make you royalty, and my heir, should you desire to be so."

Isis watched Frida intently, curious what the shy dragon's answer would be. Her colorful eyes looked deep with thought, and finally, Frida turned her snout up to face the queen and said: "Thank you... I had never known who my family was..." Her voice slowly grew more confident. "But I need to go back to Siberia, with Kostya and the frost dragons from the lab. It's where I belong and... Maybe I can even look for my mother, now that I know her name and... what she looked like."

The Dragon Queen gave her an understanding smile. "Perhaps you can finish my quest for me then— perhaps you shall find my sister." The queen extended a wing around Frida. "Just remember that you also have family here, in London. If you ever need me," she chuckled. "You know where I am."

Frida smiled in return. "Thank you. I will try my best."

The queen gave her one final nod, then spread her wings and jumped into the air. She hovered before them, and turned her sapphire eyes towards Isis. "Isis, I wish you a safe flight back to your home. If you ever need me, you too know where to find me," she bid.

"Thank you," The golden dragon answered. Isis was suddenly reminded of the dragons whose voices had been taken, and she added before the queen could fly away: "Your Majesty, I wanted to speak to you about something— Some of the dragons from the lab may be free but have been made unable to speak." She explained.

The queen listened to this, and said: "Meet me back at my court when it suits you before you make your trip home. We can discuss this with the Dragon Court and hopefully find a way to fix it."

Isis nodded. "Thank you, Your Majesty."

Finally, the Dragon Queen turned to Angus and Azara. "And both of you, thank you for your service to our species. If it hadn't been for you, we might not have won the trial. You have my personal gratitude and thanks, and my doors are always open to you as well," she said, and the green and blue dragons both answered with thankful and respectful nods.

As the Dragon Queen began to turn away, she added: "Today has been a victory. Today we have defended our rights, and put us a step closer towards equality and justice among dragons and men. We aren't quite there yet. But I believe that if we keep fighting, against people like the lab and other anti-dragonists, we will make a world where dragons and humans can coexist... As equals, not judged by appearances, by race, by species, by belief or heritage. I believe that with more dragons like the four of you... This world will come." With that, the Dragon Queen soared away into the sunset.

Isis was still so absorbed in contemplating the queen's words that she had not noticed that Frida's dual-colored eyes had turned to the ground, where Kostya had broken away from the dancing crowds and waited for her at the pavement beneath the roof. She glanced back up at Isis again. "Thank you," she repeated. "You have been an inspiration. I hope we meet again one day." With that, the delicate yet powerful dragon spread her frosty wings and glided down to the waiting arms of her adoptive father.

"Well," Azara said to Angus. "Ready to show me how to professionally ride some sheep?"

Angus grinned and nodded. "Prepare to learn some serious sheep handling skills," he joked, spreading his wings. He then paused, and rested them against his sides again. "And

Azara, I just wanted to say— You're very brave. It takes strength to tell people you have a power such as yours. I would know! And… Telempathy must make some people... Uncomfortable."

Azara gave a sad smile. "Thank you, Angus. I trust you'll keep my secret?"

His golden eyes glimmered with friendly mischevity, as if they shared some sort of secret... "For all time," he answered. This caused Azara's sad smile to burst into a full out laugh. His face then turned thoughtful. "How long have you been reading my thoughts?"

Azara tossed her head from side to side in thought. "Mmm... Sometime since you thought I was one of the most frustrating dragons on Earth? Those thoughts have a tendency of radiating. *Definitely* since the time you thought I was brilliant around the end of the trial," she said with a grin. "Though I *must* say— your mental ramblings *before* the trial gave *me* a headache!"

Now it was Angus's turn to burst out laughing. "I'll have to work on that. Though I promise you that most of the time, my head is full of sheep." He cast his glance to the setting sun. "We should be heading off," he said decidedly, spreading his golden wings for flight. "See ewe around, Isis," Angus said by means of farewell with an additional wink at his pun.

The corners of Isis's eyes crinkled. "Baaaaye baaaaye," she cordially shot back. This earned a final round of smiles from the departing dragons as they lifted off into the air. She watched as they flew off into the distance, green and blue scales sparkling in the sunset's warm golden light.

Isis watched them for a moment longer, then spread her own white wings, now glowing with all the colors of the sunset as the various colors filtered through them. She jumped off and let her wings catch the air, letting the drafts guide her. Her wings and mind free of any responsibility, any extra weight, any peril or danger or crisis... If only for a few days.

She would speak to the Dragon Queen... Then fly south. Take the long way back to Egypt... Enjoy her time to think.

Think about the dragons who'd had their voices stolen, about how they had been treated as lesser beings, just because they where... what? Smaller? She thought about these things... And how she might work to further change them...

Enjoy the flight, the freedom of the skies... Entertain the feeling of the whole, massive world for her to fly over... Free...

But she would let the warm winds guide her... Lead her back...

Back to home.

Epilogue

Mr. S stepped into the bleak grey metal room, void of everything but a white sofa and a side table; the remains of what had formerly been the break room. Poking up above the rise of the sofa he could see the wild hair of his former companion.

"The boss said that you're fired," he said casually as he stepped around the sofa towards the door at the other end of the room. When Clara persisted to be unresponsive, Mr. S continued. "After your little blunder in the courtroom— not to mention at Willough and London, I'm hardly surprised."

Still, no reaction. She just continued to stare at the doors ahead, her face bored. "It wasn't easy, you know," he pushed on. "Cleaning up the messes you made. Removing the car— that was not a simple task." He then indicated with his arms towards the general vacancy of the room. "And now thanks you to botching the whole mission up, we have to completely relocate."

Finally, Clara spoke in an annoyed but blank tone. "The London Lab was just one of many. We've got hundreds of bases around the world- I'm sure it can't be too hard to choose a new primary one."

Mr. S frowned. "London was a prime, central location. It is a severe loss for us and now we have to ship all of this tech to a new location. Did you even help disassemble The Habitats? Not to mention how much harder it's going to be to get the world leader's support now..."

Clara absentmindedly brushed some stray hairs behind her ear. "So then where are you off to now? Where is the new base?"

Mr. S raised a brow. "You really think you get to know after you've been fired? You should really consider yourself lucky that you get to live at all with all that you know." He pointed out.

Clara flung her hand out as if brushing away his words. "Well, maybe they just trust me more than you. Come on, where is it?" She insisted.

He knew he really shouldn't... But the temptation to get a stab back at her was too great. He slowly began to make his way towards the door again. "We're relocating to America," he answered casually. "I don't personally care for it, but the boss believes we can make a foothold there." He paused just before he reached the doors, waiting until they had slid open for him to add: "I'm also going to be getting a new partner. Someone efficient. Someone *sane*."

Clara initially scowled at his jibes, but then a grin tilted her lips as her gaze turned contemplative. "Well then, have fun playing with your tech toys in America. Perhaps I'll continue my work too— maybe even find a companion of my own."

Mr. S turned his back to her and started stalking through the doors, and though he wouldn't have if she had been able to see it... But he grinned. "Good luck with that, Clara," he called back to her.

He was farther along the hall now, but he could still hear her as she called: "Tell the boss I wish them well too!" Her voice was like a distant whisper in the wind now as he turned a corner.

But he could still hear her from around the bend.

"Good old Doctor Classified."

Coming soon....

Pocket Dragons 2: The Search for Will

William has been captured by the lab.
And his grandfather knows only two creatures who could possibly find him:
William's Dragons.

The pocket dragons have returned to their homelands, content in the belief that the Lab and its horrors were long behind them. Yet when William's grandfather finds Angus and Azara in Ireland, and tells them of his predicament, the dragons have to call in their friends for yet another quest:
The Search for Will.

Books by Hannah Hunley

Books In the Infinity Series:

Book One
Infinity: A Many Worlds Novel

Book Two
Infinity: Packs of Secrets

Book Three
The Midnight Star (Coming Soon)

Books in the Pocket Dragons Series:

Pocket Dragons

Pocket Dragons 2: The Search for Will (Coming Soon)

About the Author

Hannah Hunley is an award winning space cat who travels into alternate dimensions and returns to write about her adventures. She often brings home new companions, and her family is struggling to organize the menagerie of mythical creatures in their living room. It is especially hard to find room for the dragons.